ISLANDERS
ADVENTURES IN SARK

ADVENTURES OF THE ISLANDERS Volume 2

Islanders
Adventures in Sark

M.J.Vermeulen

Illustrated by the author

ELSP

First published 2010
by ELSP
16A St John's Road
St Helier
Jersey   JE2 3LD

Origination by Seaflower Books, Jersey

Printed and bound in the UK by
J F Print Ltd, Sparkford,
Somerset

ISBN 978-1-906641-23 -8

**All correspondence and enquiries regarding this book
should be addressed to the author:
M.J. Vermeulen at
Rosaire
La Mare
St Andrew's
Guernsey   GY6 8XX**

Website: islanderbooks.blogspot.com

*With special thanks to the Perrée Family
of Little Sark for their hospitality
and for helping to provide the
inspiration for this book.*

CONTENTS

WARNING

The shores, cliffs and caves of Sark are dangerous. Please keep to the paths and do not go rock climbing or caving without a properly qualified guide.

Introduction

The Islanders are a group of children who first met in Guernsey, Channel Islands, in the summer of 2008. Anna and Shani were visiting from England. A chance meeting with two local boys, Tom and Ian, led them into all sorts of adventures, during which they found Bart, the final member of the team. You can read about this in the first book *Adventures of the Islanders*.

In this sequel, the Islanders meet up again in the summer of 2009, but this time their adventures take them to Sark*, a tiny island about 8 miles off the coast of Guernsey.

Victor Hugo* described Sark as 'the most beautiful' of all the Channel Islands. He regularly stayed on Sark and found inspiration there for parts of his novel *The Toilers of the Sea*.

Many of the families on Sark can trace their roots back to the forty men who colonised the island in 1565 with the first Seigneur, Helier de Carteret, under a royal charter granted by Queen Elizabeth the first. The people of Sark are polite and friendly but they are also fiercely independent and rightly proud of their island. Sark remains relatively untouched by the modern world. It is still beautiful, wild and windswept, a magical and mysterious place, steeped in history.

Sark has been home to pirates and smugglers, its rocky shoreline riddled with secret tunnels and caves, it has been mined for silver and precious gems, it has been an artists' colony and muse to many famous poets and authors. There have been treasures found and many a shipwreck too in its sometimes treacherous waters.

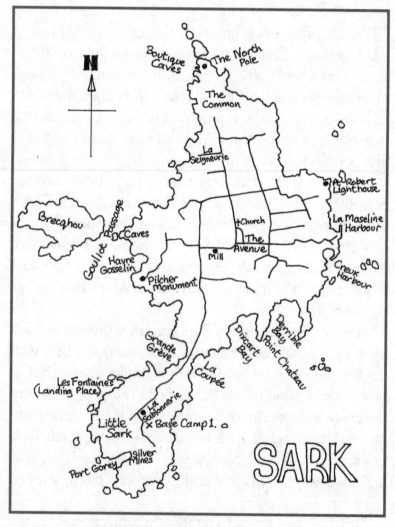

Where could we find a more perfect place for adventure,

and how better to enjoy this very special island than in the company of the Islanders? Well then, why not join them on their "Great Expedition and Exploration of Sark. GEESE for short, except we can't think of anything for the final E." It promises to be an interesting voyage, with various twists and turns and puzzling events along the way.

Chapter 1

Together Again

Tom was so excited he could hardly contain himself. He had waited so long. All through the autumn, all through the winter, all through the spring, now at last summer was here, Anna and Shani would be arriving at any minute and the Islanders would all be together again. Bart would be coming too, but nobody knew exactly when. He was helping his father to deliver a yacht and plans for his arrival had been changed at the last minute.

Best of all, Tom already knew that great adventures lay ahead of them. He could feel it in his bones. Well actually, there were other reasons why he knew that great adventures lay ahead. He could hardly believe his luck. Not only were the Islanders about to be re-united, but they would all be camping together on Sark. How about that, he said to himself.

"How about that, Ian? Sark, Ian, we're actually going to Sark!"

Tom dug Ian in the ribs, and started to tickle him.

"Gerorf!" shouted Ian, gamely defending himself.

"Honestly, Tom, I don't know what's got into you. You're like a jumping bean, a Mexican jumping bean."

"Oh come on, Ian," said Tom. "I know you're just as excited as I am. A whole week on Sark, all of us Islanders together, and Phil's taking us in *Cobo Alice*.

Cobo Alice was the name of Phil's boat, which had played an important part in their adventures of the previous summer.

"Yeah. Great isn't it?" said Ian. "I'm really looking forward to seeing the girls. I don't know what's happened to the boat though. She should be in by now, due in at half past ten."

The two boys were standing on the raised walk of the east arm of the Queen Elizabeth II marina, looking out to sea. It was a gloriously sunny day with a stiff breeze which had made the sea a little choppy. They had to shade their eyes against the sunlight sparkling on the water as they looked out towards the north where the *Condor Express* would hopefully soon appear.

"How far is it from Weymouth?" asked Tom.

"I think it's about 70 miles," said Ian. "They can do it in about two hours on a nice day."

"Blimey!" said Tom. "She can't half move." He did the maths in his head, and then counted on his fingers. "Cor, that's exactly 35 miles an hour! A lot quicker than *Cobo Alice*."

Straight ahead of them, Tom and Ian could see the islands of Herm and Jethou and beyond them, some eight miles away, the island of Sark where they would soon be setting up camp.

"I still can't believe it, Ian," said Tom. "I've only ever been to Sark once before and that was just for the day."

"Did you go for a carriage ride?" asked Ian. "That's what we did when we went over. We went for a carriage ride and then we had lunch somewhere. I can't remember where. It was great though, really lovely and peaceful, except my dad was sick on the way back."

"Was he really?" said Tom.

"Well it was pretty rough actually," said Ian. "Nearly everyone was a bit queasy."

"Come to think of it, we did go for a carriage ride," said Tom. "And we went to the Seigneurie* gardens. It's just one of those special places, Sark. I remember how quiet it was, and being really high up on the cliffs, and the lovely fresh sea air."

"I expect that's why Mrs Riley wants to take Mr Riley there," said Ian. "I reckon it'll be just the thing for him."

The trip to Sark had been suggested by Anna's parents in the first place. Mr Riley's doctor had been none too pleased with his blood pressure.

"What you need," he said, "Is complete rest, somewhere quiet, where you can get away from it all."

Mrs Riley had immediately thought of Sark. She knew how much her husband loved the islands, and surely Sark would be the ideal place for him. Traffic free, beautiful scenery and good clean air. She was quite pleased with herself at having thought of it and Mr Riley was absolutely delighted. He slapped his thigh.

"Now why didn't I think of that?" he said. "How clever

of you, my dear, but there are hardly any shops, you know. Don't you think you might get bored?"

"No, darling. This is something we have to do for you," said Mrs Riley. "You've been overdoing it of late, and you know what the doctor said. Complete rest. I think Sark will be just the place."

So they set about planning the trip.

Anna thought it was an excellent idea, but she made it clear there was no way that she and Shani were going to Sark unless the others came too.

"But what can we do, Anna?" said her mother. "You can't expect the others to pay for a week on Sark, and your father desperately needs a break."

"Don't worry about it, dear," said Mr Riley. "Remember the Tourist Board offered us a free holiday*. I shall phone them and see what can be done."

The kind people at the Tourist Board had come up with an ideal solution. Mr and Mrs Riley would have the luxury of a very quaint and comfortable hotel on Little Sark, while the children would camp out nearby. The extra numbers were no problem at all, as the overall cost would be much the same.

"I think I can see her, Tom," said Ian. "Look over there. She's just a tiny white dot on the horizon."

As they watched, slowly the dot grew bigger. They could hear the throb of the powerful engines while she was still a long way out.

"Thank goodness for that," said Tom. "I was beginning to worry Mr and Mrs Riley might miss the Sark boat.

Which one are they on, Ian? Do you know?"

"I don't think it's a problem," said Ian. "There's a boat every few hours in the summer."

Ever since the trip had been suggested Ian had made it his business to gather as much information as he could about Sark. He liked to be well prepared, and he knew what Anna was like. She would want to know everything about the place.

Tom had also been preparing for the trip with some help from his parents.

"We're going to need a tent, and sleeping bags, and maybe a camping stove," said Tom.

"And a torch," said Mrs Le Page, "And pots and pans, plates, mugs, knives and forks, and some basic provisions, just to start you off."

"Ian's bringing a lantern and his telescope, and we'll need the compass and a map for our exploring," said Tom. "I wish we had a sea chart with Sark on it. If Phil is going to take us over we could check out the rocks. Trouble is they're so expensive. I still have the one Mr Mahy gave me but it only has Guernsey and Herm on it."

"I wonder if he has any more," said Mr Le Page. "He might have you know. He said he'd given up boating, so he might have no need of them."

When he next passed that way on his bike, Tom called in to Mr Mahy's house. As always, everything was in perfect order, the lawns neatly manicured, the flower borders immaculate, and the bungalow itself looked as if it had been newly painted. Tom remembered how he had thought when he first saw the place that it looked like a ship, with its porthole windows and flagstaff.

Mr Mahy was tending one of the borders, but he saw Tom approaching and slowly raised himself up. He gradually straightened up and stretched his back.

"Hello there young feller!" he said. "Cor! This back of mine is giving me gyp today. Well, what can I do for you? You're young Tom Le Page aren't you? The young feller who had my rowing boat off me last year. How is it going by the way?"

"Very well indeed, Mr Mahy," said Tom. "We've even put a little sail up on her, and we've sailed pretty much all around Grand Havre now."

"Well I'm blowed," said Mr Mahy. "So what brings you round these parts then."

Tom explained about the trip to Sark and his quest for a sea chart. "It doesn't have to be anything special," he said, "And I'd be happy to pay you a few pounds if that's alright."

"Don't be silly," said Mr Mahy. "I heard what you and those friends of yours did last year. Good work that was. I'll be happy to look out a chart for you, and you certainly don't need to pay me for it." He trod his gardening fork into the ground and took off his gardening gloves. "Come along into the house, Tom, and we'll see what we can find."

They both walked around to the back door, wiped their feet carefully on the doormat, then Mr Mahy ushered Tom through the kitchen and into his study. The walls were covered with old paintings, prints and photographs of steamships and sailing ships, and against one of the walls stood a desk of dark polished wood with a green leather top. Mr Mahy took a roll of charts from a cupboard in the corner, laid them out on the desk, and started to sort through them.

"Here's one of Sark!" he said triumphantly. "I knew I had one somewhere, but it does look quite old, doesn't it? And it is has been a bit scribbled over I'm afraid."

Tom did not mind in the least. "That's no problem," he said. "Most of it's in pencil, and that can be rubbed out. No it's a really good one. It shows lots of the rocks and their names, and the names of the bays. It's just what I wanted. Are you sure I can't pay you something for it?"

"No, no, Tom," said Mr Mahy. "I won't be needing it now. Anyway, this lot cost me next to nothing. I bought a whole bundle of them at an auction a few years back."

"Well, that's very kind of you," said Tom. "Thank you very much. It will be just the thing for our camping trip."

"Camping in Sark is it?" said Mr Mahy. "Cor, I did that when I was a lad and didn't we have some fun. I reckon you'll enjoy it. Sark's a fine place for adventures. I made some good friends too. One of the local lads took me out shooting rabbits, and he showed us all around the caves. Sark is the place for caves you know. There's quite a few. They reckon pirates and smugglers used them in the old days. He still lives over there, this friend of mine. I'll give you his address, just in case you have time, and you can pop round perhaps and remember me to him."

Finally, Tom had managed to gather together everything on his list except the tent, which he feared might be an expensive item. Ian had the brainwave of looking for one on the internet with the help of his older sister, Emma.

"She's always looking at dresses and stuff on the internet," he said, "So she might find us a bargain. I'll try and catch her in a good mood."

In the end there was no need, as Ian's mother found an ideal two man tent on special offer in a shop in St Peter Port. It was called the High Tops Trail Tent and it cost £17.99, which shared between the two of them was not as bad as it might have been.

Anna and Shani had also been preparing for the trip. Fortunately the hotel was providing them with a tent and camp beds, so all they had to bring were sleeping bags and a few other bits and pieces in addition to their normal clothes and toiletries.

Anna had been given a watercolour painting set for Christmas, which she desperately wanted to take with her. She had read in one of the guide books that Sark was famous for its spectacular cliffs and sea views.

"The bastioned crags of the steeps of Sark," she quoted to her mother from the book. "The most beautiful spot on earth … Artists come across from the mainland for a brief holiday and stay for months."

"Well we can't stay for months, dear," said Mrs Riley, "But I'm sure the boys will help carry your paints and your easel, if you feel you have to take them."

It was a great disappointment to Anna when she read in the guide book that although there had once been stone-age megaliths and tombs on Sark, all of them had long since disappeared. There would be no archaeological adventures, so she decided that, this time, she might concentrate on her art. She pictured herself surveying the scene from a wild and windswept cliff top, the waves foaming and crashing onto the rocks below, the plaintiff cry of the gulls as they swooped and wheeled about. Shani noticed that Anna had taken to wearing a scarf and a beret in an artistic fashion.

"What time is Phil getting here?" Tom asked Ian.

"He said he would keep an eye out for the *Condor* and then make his way round."

"Here she comes," said Tom, as the *Condor Express* drew nearer.

She was a strange looking craft, very streamlined at the front, almost like a space ship, suspended over two very thin and pointy hulls that pierced through the waves. She had throttled back now and was making her way sedately between the pierheads.

"Come on, Ian. We'd better get over to the jetty and meet the girls."

"Yeah. Come on then. Race you over."

Ian and Tom climbed down from the sea wall and raced over to the jetty where Tom's father was waiting in his van reading his newspaper.

"Come on, dad. They're here!" Tom shouted breathlessly.

Bill Le Page looked up and smiled. "Right ho then," he said. "We'll go and see them come down the gang plank."

Condor Express reversed smartly up to the ramp

alongside the jetty. Ropes were led out and dropped over the bollards, and soon the gang plank was being craned into position. From behind the security fence Tom and Ian could see a queue of foot passengers forming, ready to disembark, and then they saw Mr and Mrs Riley, and Anna and Shani waving wildly.

The welcoming party waved back and watched as the passengers carefully negotiated the steep gangway down onto the quay.

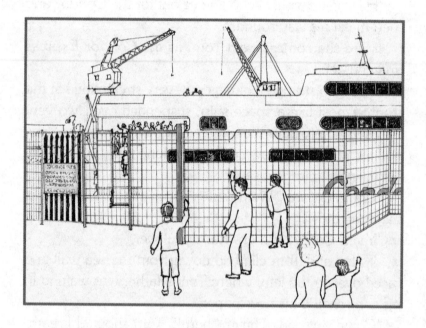

"Hello, hello! Welcome back! Lovely to see you!" they called to each other as the passengers were led off into the terminal building to collect their luggage.

Just a few minutes later the Rileys, with daughter and friend, emerged from the building pushing a large trolley piled high with suitcases, bundles and bags, to be greeted with much enthusiasm, hugs and laughter by the others. There was a great babble as everyone tried to speak at once, then more hugs and laughter.

"Good to see you!" said Bill Le Page. "Did you have a good trip?"

"Wonderful thank you," said Mrs Riley.

"Relatively smooth, just a slight chop," said Mr Riley, "But you know, the view of St Peter Port as you draw closer is magnificent. I shall never tire of it."

The boys and girls were soon in earnest discussion, checking the final details of their trip, "The Great Expedition and Exploration of Sark," as Bart had named it (GEESE for short except they could not think of anything suitable for the final E).

"Do you know where Bart is?" Tom asked Anna.

"Yes, I'll tell you later. What about Phil?"

"He should be here any minute."

"Where are we going to meet him?"

"Over there. There's a slipway where my dad can drive down with the van."

"Oh, it's so lovely to be back together again," said Shani. "Now I feel like a proper Islander again."

"Yeah! Islanders forever!" said Ian and Tom together.

Chapter 2

Landing on Sark

Mr and Mrs Riley decided to stay in St Peter Port for lunch, and then leave for Sark on the 2.30pm boat. They left their luggage at the Sark Shipping office and headed off into Town.

The boys helped Anna and Shani to stow their luggage in the back of Bill Le Page's van, and then there was just about room for the four of them to squeeze in for the short trip over to the slipway.

"There he is," said Bill Le Page as he reversed down, "Just coming in now."

The back doors of the van were flung open and the four passengers tumbled out onto the slipway. Anna and Shani, especially, couldn't wait to see Phil and *Cobo Alice*.

The little fishing boat had slowed right down some thirty metres away while Phil put out the fenders, ready to come alongside. He waved back as the children waved and shouted out their greetings. Then he brought *Cobo Alice* smartly up to the edge of the slipway and tossed a rope to each of the boys who made them fast to some metal rings.

"Hello my fellow Islanders!" said Phil.* "It's great to see you again girls. Now we're nearly up to full strength. What's happened to young Bart then?"

"Sailing over from St Malo," said Tom. "He's going to meet us in Sark."

"He sent us a text," said Anna. "Hopefully, his father will drop him off some time tomorrow."

"A text? I didn't know Bart had a mobile phone," said Tom.

"Yes. His mother gave it to him for his birthday. She was hoping it might help him to keep in touch while he's gadding about here there and everywhere," said Anna.

"Anyway, it's great 'cos we can text each other now."

"Right. Come on you lot," said Bill Le Page. "There's all this stuff to get onboard."

They formed a chain and passed the luggage over to Ian and Phil onboard *Cobo Alice* who stowed everything carefully in the bows of the boat and finally covered it with a tarpaulin.

The explorers said their farewells to Bill Le Page, thanking him profusely for all his help and took their places onboard the fishing boat. Phil started the engine, gave the order to cast off, and reversed smoothly away from the slipway. The fenders were brought in, the helm swung over, and *Cobo Alice* made a graceful pirouette and headed out towards the marina gates.

They chugged along past row upon row of white plastic pleasure boats. Huge and expensive though some of them were, it seemed to the children that not one of them was half as nice as Phil's boat. Anna thought it almost felt as if *Cobo Alice* was laughing at the other boats as she burbled skittishly and happily along. Poor things! They hardly ever went out, but *Cobo Alice* was out fishing nearly every day.

Bill Le Page gave them a last wave as they finally disappeared from sight. They passed over the sill of the marina gate and cleared the outer breakwater, then Phil pushed the throttle lever forwards and headed out, virtually due east, towards the islands of Herm and Jethou. Out on the open sea the boat took on a different character, eagerly punching forwards and riding the waves.

"Are we going through the passage between Herm and Jethou?" Shani asked Phil.

"Not this time, my love," said Phil. "We'll take the Tobars passage, just south of Jethou. Might save us a few minutes, and you'll get a nice view of the island too."

"How long will it take us to get to Sark?" asked Anna.

"Ooh, 'bout an hour or so," said Phil. "You're staying on Little Sark, aren't you? So I'm going to drop you off at the Fontaine. That'll be a good place to land on this tide, and you'll be nice and close to the hotel."

"This is kind of you, Phil, to take us over," said Anna.

"No problem at all," said Phil. "As a matter of fact I've a few pots to lift on my way back, so it'll work out fine."

Tom had taken out his chart of Guernsey, Herm and Sark. He was looking for the Tobars passage.

"That looks like an old one," said Phil.

"Yes, I was wondering, Phil," said Tom, "If you had any

idea what all these lines and numbers are for."

Phil let Anna steer the boat while he looked at the chart. "Keep her at 90 degrees," he said. "You have to keep that beacon on Grande Fauconniere just sitting on top of the south slope of Jethou. That's it, steady as she goes. Now let me see."

He took the chart and studied it carefully, turning it this way and that. "Don't have much use for charts myself," he chuckled. "I tend to steer by the seat of my pants."

After quite some time he handed the chart back to Tom. "Makes no sense to me at all," he said. "Don't look like fishing marks, and they don't look like a course to steer neither. I can't think what they might mean. Sorry, Tom."

Tom was quite surprised by this. He had been sure that Phil would be able to explain it all to him.

Cobo Alice was now approaching Jethou. "Right ho, Anna. Just hold her steady for a minute," said Phil as he turned and peered aft into the distance. He lifted his hand to his brow, shielding his eyes from the sun. "Now, you see Brehon Tower there? We have to wait till it lines up with the Vale Mill just showing to the left of it..... OK, take her to starboard now, right hand down, that's it, hold her there, should be about 140 degrees on the compass."

Anna was having a wonderful time being the helmsman. "Aye aye, sir. 140 degrees it is."

"Now the next bit is quite easy," said Phil. "As soon as you can see Noir Pute, you just head straight for it, leaving Grande Fauconniere to port. We can go quite close if you like."

"But where is Noir Pute, and what is it?" said Anna, panicking slightly.

"You'll see it in a minute," said Phil. "It's a black rock, right in the middle of the Russel*, well east of Herm.

"I've got it," said Tom. "Here it is on the chart, Anna."

While Tom and Anna steered the boat, Ian and Shani were enjoying the ever changing scene around them, the sea-birds resting on the rocks as they passed close by, the view of Guernsey behind them getting smaller and smaller as they drew further away, and the rocky shores and steep slopes of Jethou and Grande Fauconniere. Now, as they rounded Jethou, they could see Sark before them with its offshore island of Brecqhou in front.

"About another four or five miles to go," said Phil, as they chugged past the Fourquies buoy and altered course towards their destination. "See those arrows on top of the buoy?" said Phil. "Twin arrows pointing upwards. That means it's a north cardinal buoy. You have to pass on the north side of it."

As they drew closer to Brecqhou, Phil eased back on the throttle so they could have a better view of the castle. "What d'you think of that then?" he said.

"Isn't it beautiful," said Shani. "Is it very old, Phil?"

Phil laughed. "You wouldn't think it would you, but it was only built a few years ago. Cor they've spent some money on that place alright. There's the castle itself, and all the roads and the harbour, and landscaped gardens on the top and all sorts."

Cobo Alice chugged happily on past Brecqhou and

around through the narrow passage separating the island from mainland Sark, then they headed south towards Little Sark. They marvelled at the cliffs towering above them, deeply cracked and fissured, the glowing colours of the rocks and flowers clinging to the slopes, and the sea so blue and so clear. Ian was especially fascinated by the rock formations, which were quite different from anything he had seen in Guernsey, such dramatic shapes.

"I reckon some of the rock must have been really soft," he said, "And that's got washed away by the sea, and what we're left with is all these amazing shapes."

"And all the caves as well," said Tom.

"It's just such a perfect place to be an artist," said Anna happily. "I can't wait to get started."

"Right. We have to head out a bit now, to clear some of that rubbish," said Phil, pointing at some rocks which were just showing above the water. "Then we'll head into the Fontaine. It's just past that big rock over there, the Baveuse."

They rounded the Baveuse and found themselves entering a natural harbour with jagged rocks around its outer edge providing shelter. The engine was throttled back and *Cobo Alice* slid gently to a halt.

"Now we'll just need this old calyx," said Phil, reaching for a strange device that looked rather like an old TV aerial. It was a length of galvanized pipe with steel rods sticking through its lower end, the top being connected to a length of chain and rope. He lowered the calyx over the side, paid out the chain and rope, and then twisted and tugged at it until he was sure it was holding fast. "Boulders on the bottom here," he said. "The old calyx holds best, and I ain't too worried if she gets stuck. I can always make another one."

With *Cobo Alice* safely moored, the next job was to ferry the explorers and their equipment over to the landing place.

"It'll be good rowing practice for you," said Phil.

"Can Shani and I have a go as well please?" said Anna.

"Don't see why not," said Phil, untying the painter of the tender, "But we'll just watch the boys first and see how they get on. Ian, you can go first. I know you can row pretty well. Tom, you get in with Ian and I'll pass in some of your gear."

The two boys climbed carefully into the tender, which was a little flat bottomed boat made of plywood, brightly painted in blue and yellow. The cargo was stowed in the bow, Tom sat in the stern, and Ian took the oars.

"Over there," said Phil, pointing to a gully with an area of flat rocks to one side. "That's the landing place. Mind how you go now."

Anna and Shani watched as Ian and Tom rowed steadily towards the gully.

"It's our turn next!" said Shani.

The tender reached the landing place. Ian shipped the oars while Tom grabbed the rocks and held the tender tightly alongside. It was actually quite tricky stepping off onto the rocks. He had to time it in between waves, then at just the right moment he leapt ashore. Sadly for Tom, although the timing was right, the rocks on which he landed were covered in some very slippery seaweed. His feet shot out from underneath him and, arms flailing, hopelessly trying to regain his balance, he fell and landed with a bellow and a splash in a sitting position. Amazingly, he still managed to hang onto the painter so that the tender did not drift away.

"Are you okay, Tom?" said Ian.

"Not exactly, Ian," said Tom. "I seem to be sitting in a puddle, and my bottom parts are completely soaked."

"Oooh, Tom. That must be really uncomfortable," said Ian, breaking into a giggle.

"Yes it's alright for you, Ian," said Tom struggling to his feet and trying to wring some of the wetness out of his shorts, "Sitting in your nice, dry, comfortable boat." But Tom could see the funny side as well and they both had to laugh about it.

When they had regained their composure, Ian passed over the equipment and made ready to return. Luckily, Tom's rucksack was included in the first load, so he was able to change out of his wet shorts while Ian rowed back.

"I don't think we should let the girls have a go, do you, Tom? I think it's probably a bit too dangerous. I'll have a word with them when I get back," said Ian, heading out into the bay, "But don't worry, Tom," he said, breaking into another fit of the giggles, "I won't tell them about your little accident."

In view of the slippery conditions at the landing place, Phil decided that perhaps it would be safer if Ian ferried the girls and the remaining equipment across, and when they reached the landing place Tom was there to help them unload. On the last trip Tom was sufficiently recovered to row out, and Phil rowed back with him and gave them directions for the hotel. "Just follow the path up. It'll take you straight there," he said. "See you next week for the trip back. Have a great time on Sark!"

The landing party waved him off. Tom was quite excited now they were safely on Sark.

"Islanders forever!" he shouted, jumping up and down.

"Islanders forever!" Phil called back and gave them a wave.

"We're marooned," said Anna. "Marooned on a desert

island."

They gathered their luggage together and, heavily laden, picked their way carefully over the rocks.

"Mind out! These rocks are slippery, eh Tom?" said Ian.

They reached the steep path which led up towards the cliff top. A little way up the path they turned to watch as Phil boarded *Cobo Alice*, started her up, and hoisted the calyx, which had held fast and required a few twists and tugs this way and that before it came free.

They waved Phil off as *Cobo Alice* chugged out of the natural harbour of La Fontaine and set a course for Guernsey.

The view from the path was quite magnificent. A huge expanse of blue sea stretched out to the west, mostly calm, but here and there whipped into wavelets and tidal eddies. Close in: the jagged rocks and steep slopes of Sark, clothed in greenery, flowers of pink and white and the yellow gorse; further out: Herm and Jethou, some 5 or 6 miles away, with Guernsey beyond in the distance.

"I don't know about a desert island. It feels more like Treasure Island to me," said Shani.

"It's just so magical," said Anna. "To think only a few hours ago we were in dreary old England, and now we are here in this tropical paradise."

"More like sub-tropical really," said Ian.

"On a good day," said Tom.

They spent a few minutes watching *Cobo Alice* getting smaller and smaller as she made her way out across the Great Russel, and taking in the beauty of their new surroundings. It was so quiet. All they could hear was the putt putt of her engine.

"Treasure Island. Ahaarr me hearties!" said Tom, getting into pirate mode, and then he broke into song*:

> "Fifteen men on a dead man's chest,
> Yo ho ho and a bottle of rum,
> Drink and the devil had done for the rest,
> Yo ho ho and a bottle of rum."

"Hey, that's really good, Tom," said Shani. "Can you teach us the words?"

"That's all I know," said Tom. I've forgotten the rest."

Chapter 3

Setting up Camp

They continued their climb up the steep path until they eventually came to a fork.

"Which one shall we take?" asked Ian. "Phil said the path just led straight to the hotel."

"Perhaps they both do," said Anna. "Eeny meeny miney mo. Let's take that one."

They took the path on the left and after a while they reached the top of the cliff where, after various twists and turns, they came upon a tiny little stone cottage, painted white with a red roof of corrugated iron.

"Wait!" Anna hissed, motioning with her hand for them to stop.

They dropped down and peered ahead of them to see what was wrong. Then they saw that the front door had opened and a very old lady had emerged, bent nearly double over a broom, which actually looked very much like a witch's broomstick. Anna turned to the others, wide eyed.

"I don't believe it," she whispered. "Look over there.

She's got a black cat as well."

They did not know quite what to do. Surely she could not really be a witch? But regardless of that, they felt embarrassed that they might have taken the wrong path and ended up in someone's private property.

The old lady was busy sweeping and talking to her cat in a funny sing-song kind of voice. She stopped for a moment and looked over in their direction, then she carried on sweeping and the children thought perhaps she had not seen them. Maybe they should just sneak off, go back and take the other path. They skulked off around the corner. As soon as they were a safe distance from the cottage they all tried to whisper at once.

"Did you see that ... She had a big hooked nose ...

And did you see her clothes? They were like something from the olden days … Yes, and the black cat … and the witch's broomstick."

It was only Ian who sounded slightly more sensible.

"That's probably how it is on Sark. There's not many shops, so probably you have to make your own brooms and things. And anybody can have a black cat. There's nothing odd about that."

They reached the fork and took the other path which led them across some fields and through a tiny hamlet of quaint little cottages, quite similar to the one they had seen on the cliffs. Then they followed a wider track which took them up to the hotel. On the way, Tom was thinking about the old lady and what Ian had said.

"Do you think we should go back and say hello?" he said. "What if she did see us? She might think we were a bit weird creeping off like that."

"You're right, Tom," said Shani.

"We can always go back tomorrow," said Anna.

They reached the gate leading into the hotel gardens.

"Wow. Mother and father will love this," said Anna.

The gardens were immaculate, with beautifully tended lawns and flower borders, and paths of fine red gravel sculpted and swept to perfection, so that they hardly dared walk over them. The hotel itself was a picturesque collection of old buildings, converted barns and stables scattered around and about. They reached an entrance porch with an open door leading into a dark interior, but it seemed there was no one there, no noise or sign of anyone. Ian and Tom sat down on a wooden bench to take the weight off. It had been quite a climb up from the Fontaine with all of their luggage.

Anna peeked inside the door. "Oh look," she said, "Isn't this lovely."

When her eyes had become accustomed she found a charming, comfortably furnished room, with low tables and chairs, blackened beams, a huge open fireplace, and to one side a bar with all sorts of drinks and glasses along the back wall.

Wondering whether she should actually be in the bar, she walked outside again, just in time to meet the manageress who had happened past and seen the bags and Shani waiting at the door.

"Can I help you?" she said.

"I hope we've come to the right place," said Shani.

"Yes. This is the Sablonnerie isn't it?" said Anna. "We're supposed to be camping here. My parents are arriving later."

"Well goodness me! You must be the Rileys. We weren't expecting you so soon," said the lady. "How did you get here so quickly?"

The children told her about Phil and their trip on *Cobo Alice*.

"Oh yes. I know Phil," said the lady. "So you landed at the Fontaine. Gosh. Nobody's done that for years. Well you're very welcome. Can I get you some drinks? Some lemonade perhaps or a coke, and then I'll show you where you can make camp. We don't normally allow camping you know, but when we heard what very special people you were...well...we thought we'd better make an exception."

When they had finished their drinks, the lady from the hotel, or Mrs B, as she asked to be called, led them across the garden, through a gap in a bamboo hedge, and down a rough path through some trees until they reached a clearing.

"I know what it's like when you're camping," she said. "You don't want to be too close to civilization. What do you think of it?"

"It's perfect," said Anna. "Just perfect, thank you."

"The path over there leads to the silver mines and Venus pool," said Mrs B. And that one over there...Oh never mind. I'll let you find out for yourselves. It'll be more fun. Right, if this is OK for you, I'll find someone to bring over the tent and the camp beds."

"We'll come and fetch them if you like," said Anna.

"Fair enough," said Mrs B, "If you're sure its not too much trouble."

"No trouble at all," said Anna, who was very impressed by Mrs B and her understanding of what was needed for the perfect campsite.

"We'll stay here and start unpacking," said Ian.

On the way back to the hotel Mrs B showed the girls where the nearest tap was, to fill their water bottles, and talked to them about various places they might like to visit in Sark.

"Did you say something earlier about the silver mines?" asked Anna.

"The silver mines," said Mrs B. "Oh yes, not much to see now but there's quite a story attached to those.

You should speak to our neighbour, Mr Elwood. He's an expert on them. Oh, and there's a plan of them in the hotel, showing all the different levels. It's on the wall in the restaurant. Have a look later on if you're having dinner there."

They came to a small wooden shed near the back door of the hotel.

"Just hang on to these will you," said Mrs B, as she passed out a large brown tent bag and two folding beds.

"Silver mines! That sounds really exciting doesn't it Shani?" said Anna.

"Yes, we'll have to go exploring," said Shani. "They might have left a few nuggets behind. It will be like searching for buried treasure!"

Mrs B laughed. "Oh yes, there are all sorts of treasures to be found. Do you know about Sarkstone?"

"Do you mean the local granite?" said Anna.

"No, not the local granite... Sark amethyst," said Mrs B. "It's a beautiful purple gemstone. They used to mine it over here. And I've heard of other gemstones too. People have been known to find them on Grande Grève at low tide."

"Oh, my goodness!" said Shani, in amazement. "We've just so much to do. Silver mines, and now precious jewels as well."

"Come on," said Mrs B. "I'll give you a hand to carry these back.

Ian and Tom had been sorting through the luggage.

"There's not much we can do," said Ian, "Until the girls come back with their tent."

"We could put up our tent," said Tom, holding up the

bright blue bag that contained the High Tops Trail Tent.

"Yeah. Let's see if we can put it up before they get back," said Ian.

So they emptied the bag and got to work as quickly as they could.

"Lucky we've been camping before," said Tom, "So we know where all the pieces go."

Five minutes later the boys were inside the tent, wrestling with the poles and ridge pieces, when Mrs B and the girls turned up.

"No, Tom," said Ian. "Pass me that bit with the plastic end. That must be part of the ridge. I'm sure the poles can't be that high."

"Oh dear," said Mrs B. "Look at that. It seems that your camp has been invaded by some kind of blue monster, which, sadly, has eaten those two nice boys who came with you."

The wobbling mass of blue canvas started to laugh, collapsed completely, and then a few seconds later two red faces emerged, of two slightly embarrassed boys.

"I know what's happened," said Shani. "They've been trying to do it without the instructions!"

"Typical," said Mrs B. "Here, let me see if I can sort you out."

Within a few minutes, under the direction of Mrs B, the tent stood straight and true in the centre of the clearing.

"Now it's starting to look more like a campsite," said Mrs B. "Gosh, I almost wish I was sleeping here myself tonight. There's nothing like sleeping under canvas. But the old bones wouldn't take too kindly to it. Now, do you think you can manage the other one by yourselves? It's very simple really. Just like the little one, except the poles are made of wood."

"I'm sure we can manage, thank you," said Ian.

"Right ho then, I'll leave you to it. Come around to the hotel when you're ready. Your elders should be arriving pretty soon, but don't worry, I'll keep them entertained until you get there."

"Thanks ever so much, Mrs B," said Anna and Shani.

"Yes, thank you for all your help," said Tom and Ian.

"No need to thank me," said Mrs B, bustling off towards the hotel, "I've really enjoyed it."

"Isn't she great?" said Anna. "If everyone here is like that, I think we're going to have a really nice holiday."

"Yes, and do you know, boys, Mrs B has been telling Anna and me about the silver mines, and Sark amethysts, and where to find precious jewels washed up on the beaches," said Shani.

"Cor, Sark is just amazing," said Tom. "There's just so much we have to explore!"

They set to and pitched the hotel's brown tent next to the blue one, and put up the camp beds inside.

"This is nice and roomy," said Tom. "It's about twice the size of ours. You sure you don't want to swap?"

"No way," said Anna. "This is just as it should be. Us charming young ladies in this grand tent, and you ruffians in the little, humble tent."

"Absolutely," said Shani, sticking her nose in the air.

"Oooh! Hoity toity!" laughed Tom.

He was tying back the side flaps of the doorway, and he

looked at the huge amount of luggage just outside which the girls had brought with them.

"Anyway, by the time you get that lot inside, it won't be quite so roomy then."

"Hey, girls," said Ian, changing the subject, "Did Mrs B say anything about the old lady on the cliffs?"

"No, we didn't ask her," said Anna.

"I don't suppose she is a witch really," said Shani.

"Maybe we should go and say hello," said Anna. "It must be lonely for her, living all by herself on the cliff top."

"We don't know for sure that she lives alone," said Ian. "There might be someone else living with her."

They just about managed to find space for everything inside the tents and then stood outside to admire their handiwork.

"Just one thing missing," said Ian. "We need a flagstaff for our flag."

They hunted amongst the trees and soon found a suitable fallen branch from which they prized off a nice straight piece about 2 metres long. Tom managed to dig a small hole with his penknife, to take the base of the flagstaff, and they used some stones for extra support. Then, with some ceremony, Tom produced the new Islanders flag, tied it at the top, and they all stood to attention while Anna said a few words.

"I name this camp: Islanders Base Camp 1, in the Great Expedition and Exploration of Sark, and I wish us all, each and every one of us, much success in our adventures."

There was polite applause.

"The flag looks lovely, Tom. Well done," said Shani.

Chapter 4

La Sablonnerie

Mr and Mrs Riley had a very pleasant lunch in one of the town restaurants overlooking the harbour. Mr Riley was feeling more and more relaxed. The worries of work and life in the city would soon be forgotten, for the time being at least, and he was already starting to feel more like his old self. Mrs Riley could see the difference in him.

"This is just the start, Ted," she said, reaching out and taking his hand. "Wait till we get you to Sark."

The trip on the Sark boat had been a straightforward affair that took some 50 minutes or so, through the Percée passage between Herm and Jethou, across the Russel and around the northern tip of Sark, past the Point Robert lighthouse and into Maseline harbour.

A row of tractors and trailers awaited them on the pier, with the drivers calling out the names of their hotels.

"Sablonnerie! Over here thank you. Nice to see you. Mr and Mrs Riley is it?"

A strong young man with a ruddy outdoor complexion

and a mop of dark hair grabbed their cases and threw them up into the trailer as if they weighed next to nothing.

"You're not expecting me to travel in that trailer I hope?" said Mrs Riley, somewhat nervously.

"No, madam," laughed the young man. "There's a proper trailer with seats, just through the tunnel there, which will take you up the hill. Then you can take a carriage, or hire bikes, or walk if you like, just as you please."

There was quite a hustle and bustle about the place, as dozens of visitors alighting from the boat jostled with similar numbers of passengers boarding, all of their suitcases and bags being loaded and unloaded by hand. Mr Riley thought that some of those leaving the island looked a little sad. Poor things, they were going home, whereas he had just arrived. He took a deep breath of fresh sea air.

"Come along, darling," he said. "Let's walk shall we?"

Mrs Riley smiled and took his arm as they strode off together through the tunnel that led to the foot of harbour hill.

They took their time climbing the hill, taking a separate path to one side, and when they finally reached the top they stopped off for refreshments at a quaint little tearoom before continuing their journey to Little Sark.

Back at the camp site, the Islanders had decided it would probably be ages before the grown-ups arrived so they might as well get on with some exploring. They took the path leading away from the hotel as it seemed so much more appealing to be heading away from civilization. After a few twists and turns through the woods they emerged into bright sunlight and a wide open vista of green fields and blue skies. They skirted around the first field and found a gateway leading to a wider, dusty track, which headed south towards the cliffs.

"You couldn't really get lost in Little Sark could you?" said Shani. "You'd soon find the cliffs and you can follow them around until you reach somewhere that you know where you are."

"Yes," said Tom, looking doubtful. "I think that makes sense."

"That's why it's called Little Sark," said Ian, as they were getting closer to the cliff top, "Because it's only little."

"Mmmm," said Tom, teasing as usual and nodding his head. "That seems fairly obvious, Ian."

"There's nothing small about the cliffs though," said Anna, as they reached the edge. "Just look at the view from here."

They found themselves lost for words, their senses made giddy by the great height and the stunning scene laid out before them. Across a vast expanse of sea to the south they could see Jersey, and to the west, Herm and Jethou with Guernsey beyond. Looking east they could just make out parts of the coast of France. Around the southern tip of Sark the deep blue sea was studded with islets and rocks fringed in white breaking surf, and immediately before them, down to their left, cutting deep into the island, a sheltered cove where a boat lay at anchor, so far below that she looked like a tiny toy.

Tom broke the silence as usual. "Looks like a fishing boat of some sort," he said. "Let's have a look through the telescope, Ian. I think I can see some people on board."

Ian passed over the telescope and Tom trained it on the boat.

"She's quite big actually. They're just lowering a dinghy over the side. Looks like she's French. She's flying the tricoleur."

"Yeah, it's only about twenty miles to France from here," said Ian. "I expect they have quite a few French boats calling in."

"Cor, it must be great to sail over from France and have a whole bay to yourselves to anchor in like that," said Tom. "Oh, that reminds me, any news from Bart?"

"No, nothing as yet," said Anna, checking her phone. Shall I send him another text?"

"Yes. Let him know we've arrived in Sark, and we're waiting for him," said Shani.

"Ok. Arrived...Sark...full stop," said Anna, as she texted. "No wait a minute, I'll change that. GEESE have landed... full stop. Any news? Send to...Bart...Ok, it's gone."

Tom had brought his chart and was looking again at all the lines and numbers scrawled on it. "Here, I can see there's a line leading from that island over there, called L'Etac, and there's another one leading to that rock over there," he said, pointing to a rock some ways offshore and checking it against his chart. "They must mean something, but I don't know what."

"I wonder if Mrs B might know," said Anna. "She seems to be a mine of information."

"Talking of mines," said Ian, pointing to the other side of the cove. "I wonder if that's the ruins of the silver mines."

Looking carefully, they could just make out the ruins which Ian had noticed. Then Tom spotted something, further in to their left, which looked like the remains of a high tower or a chimney.

Shani had edged her way carefully a little further towards the cliff edge. "Hey," she said, "There's a path just below us, leading down to the bay. Shall we have a closer look?"

"No," said Ian. "I think we should find out some more about the mines first. It'll be more fun exploring if we know what we're looking for."

"Well, I know what I'm looking for," said Tom. "It's nearly 4 o'clock and I'm famished. Let's head back to base camp shall we?"

Everyone laughed. "Still the same old Tom," said Shani.

"Is it really 4 o'clock?" said Anna. "Crumbs, we'd better be getting back anyway. No doubt mother and father will have arrived, and mother will be wanting to check on us. I suppose we'd better try to get off to a good start. We don't want to be grounded on our first day!"

They arrived back at the hotel, at about quarter past four, to find Mr and Mrs Riley sitting at a table in the rose garden enjoying afternoon tea.

"Well, there you are," said Mr Riley. "Draw up a

chair. Come and join us, do. We chose a large table especially."

"Now boys," said Mrs Riley. "You must try some of these scones with Sark cream and home made jam. They are delicious."

"If you're sure you don't mind, Mrs Riley," said Tom.

"We have brought our own provisions," said Ian.

"Nonsense," said Mrs Riley. "You are to eat with us as part of the family. Isn't that so, Edward?"

"Indeed it is," said Mr Riley, "And we won't hear otherwise."

There were times when Mr Riley could be quite firm, and Tom and Ian could see there was no point in discussing the matter further.

Mrs Riley was quite right about the scones. They were home made and light as a feather. The jam was sweet and syrupy, made with blackberries from the cliffs of Little Sark, and the cream rich and thick from the cows that grazed its fields.

After tea, Tom and Ian were able to talk to Mrs B. Tom showed her the chart with all the marks and notes on it.

"They look like compass bearings, don't they," said Mrs B. "Goodness me! How untidy. It's difficult to make any sense of it." She thought for a moment. "I know who you need to talk to about this. My cousin Robert. He does the boat trips around the island. There's nothing he doesn't know about navigation and charts and all that sort of thing. I'll tell you where to find him, and I'll phone him later on to let him know you'll be coming to see him. He's also one of our special constables, you know. And the silver mines? Yes, you should really have a look at the old print in the restaurant, and another place where you will find all sorts of information, of course, is the tourist office. In fact, I'll fetch a map from reception and mark both of those places on it for you. Bob's place and the tourist office. Is that ok?"

"Yes, thank you," said the boys.

"Now we're really getting somewhere," said Tom, as Mrs B hurried off to find a map. "If the local boatman can't help us, then nobody can."

The rest of the day passed pleasantly enough. There was no time for more exploring. Mr and Mrs Riley wanted to chat with Ian and Tom about how things were in Guernsey.

Later on Ian and Tom returned to the camp to tidy themselves up before dinner.

"I haven't brought anything smart enough to wear in the restaurant, have you Ian?" said Tom.

"Not really," said Ian. "I thought we would be eating around the camp fire. Tell you what though. If we keep one pair of shorts and a clean shirt for best, and wear the other stuff for exploring, that's about all we can do. And what are we going to do with our provisions, Tom? "

Tom looked at the loaf of bread, biscuits, the tins of corned beef, beans and sausages and various soups they had brought with them. "Maybe we can have the occasional snack if we get hungry during the day," he said. "We're bound to work up an appetite with all the exploring we're going to do."

By the time they arrived back at the hotel, all of the

guests were gathering in the bar, for drinks before dinner. There was a tremendous din as everyone seemed to be in good humour and more than happy to chat with everyone else. Menus were passed around and discussed, choices made, and eventually each party was called in turn to their table in the restaurant.

The food was delicious but Tom and Ian were not fully able to relax and enjoy their meal as they had seen, on the wall opposite, the old print showing the layout of the silver mines. Anna and Shani had seen it too and, after they had eaten the first course, Anna asked Mrs Riley if they could go and look at it.

"Certainly not," said Mrs Riley. "You must wait until everyone has finished before you leave the table."

This caused great unrest amongst the explorers, but they realized they would have to wait. In fact, Tom and Ian were much better behaved than the girls, who became somewhat restless and mischievous during the meal, trying to distract them by making faces and prodding them under the table. Finally, dinner was finished and they were allowed to leave the table and gather around the ancient picture, which showed the various shafts and levels of the mines.

"Good gracious!" said Mr Riley, who had also been dying to examine it more closely. "I had no idea they had mined on such a large scale. It looks as if there were five, or is it six levels? And some of them stretched out under the sea. I wouldn't have fancied that much, the thought of that huge weight of water above me."

The children were eventually allowed to drag

themselves away and head off to their camp.

"Ye gods, that was awful," said Anna. "I hope we don't have to go through that every night. We haven't even had a chance to make plans for tomorrow."

"It wasn't that bad," said Tom. "And it's actually very kind of your parents to treat us."

"Yes, I know," said Anna, "But the thought of having to make small talk with the parents every night! How on earth are we going to have any adventures with them breathing down our necks."

"Well, we're here now," said Shani, as they arrived back at the camp. "So what shall we do tomorrow?"

"Anything from Bart yet?" asked Ian.

"No, not a thing," said Anna. "I'll leave it for now though, and try him again first thing tomorrow. But after breakfast I'm going out on the cliffs to do some painting. I've been dying to make a start."

"Okay," said Ian. "While you do that, provided we don't have to meet Bart, I reckon the rest of us might as well go to the tourist office to find out some more about the silver mines."

"And the Sark amethysts," said Shani.

"And the caves, and anything else," said Tom. "I reckon there are going to be all sorts of things to explore."

"And we have to see Mrs B's cousin, Robert."

"Right, but I want to come with you for that," said Anna. "Just give me a couple of hours and then we can meet up somewhere before lunch. I don't want to miss out on any exploring."

It was starting to get quite dark, and they noticed how

the night sky had filled with stars, so many more than usual, and how much more brightly they shone.

"I don't think I have ever seen anything more beautiful," said Shani.

"The more you look, the more you can see," said Ian.

"Och, Aye!" said Tom, in his best Scots accent, "It's a braw, bricht, moonlicht nicht, the noo!"

Anna and Shani laughed. "Tom, you are completely barking mad," said Shani.

To which Tom replied with his impression of a dog howling at the moon.

It was starting to get chilly. Ian lit the lantern so they could see their way into the tents, and they all said goodnight. Anna and Shani settled down quite comfortably on their camp beds, and Ian and Tom less comfortably on their thin sleeping mats.

"Blimey, this ground's hard as a rock," said Tom.

But despite the hardness of the ground, and the excitement of the day, they were tired and were soon fast asleep.

Chapter 5

The Stranger at Cliff Cottage

Anna looked at her watch. Six o'clock. Oh no! She had been awake for ages, or at least it felt as if she had been. Beams of bright sunlight shone in through the gaps around the door of the tent. She looked over at Shani. Fast asleep. That girl would sleep through the end of the world, she thought. Well, I might as well get started, no way I'll get back to sleep now. If I finish painting early, I can go with the others to the tourist office

She quietly pulled on her clothes while sitting in bed, gathered her painting gear and slipped out into the fresh morning air. She scribbled a note. "Gone painting, back at 8 (ish)," and signed it "A." She took a drawing pin from her painting set, and pinned the note to the flagstaff. Then she set off in the direction of the Fontaine. The dew was still wet on the path, but luckily the grass was short and her shoes did not get too wet if she trod carefully.

She reached the point where the path forked, left for the Fontaine, right for the cottage where they had seen the old lady. I wonder if she might be up and about, thought Anna. She walked a little way up the path until the cottage came into view, and as she approached she noticed a wisp of pale grey smoke coming from the chimney, almost white against the deep blue sky. Good, she thought. The old lady must be in. Better get it over and done with, just to let her know they had meant no harm. She walked up the garden path and met the black cat, sunning itself in the porch. "Hello puss," she said, going to stroke it. The cat stood up, stretched, and arched its back as she ran her hand over it. "My, you're a nice well fed puss aren't you?" she said, and tickled under its chin. But the cat didn't care for this much, and it pulled away and darted out of the porch. Anna straightened and went to knock at the door, but before she could do so the door opened and a voice came out, but it was not the voice she had been expecting.

"Yes. Vot is it?"

She blinked in surprise and looked up at a man standing half behind the door. He was tall and thin with a sallow complexion and a stubble beard. He was holding a sheaf of papers in one hand and she noticed his fingers were stained with nicotine.

"Oh, I'm sorry," she said. "I've come to see ... well er, yesterday we saw an old lady in the garden, and we thought she must live here."

"Yes, that is right. The old lady. Vot do you vant?"

Anna was so taken by surprise that she did not know what to say.

"It's just that ..."

"Come on," said the man, "Vee haf not got all day."

He spoke with a guttural accent which Anna could not quite place.

"I'm sorry," she said. "It's just that we were here yesterday, and we were just worried that we might have frightened her."

"We ... who is we?" said the man.

"The four of us," said Anna.

"Oh, I see," said the man. "Children playing tricks? You like to frighten old ladies?"

"No, no. It was nothing really," said Anna. "Is she at home? I would just like to say hello."

"I tell her you call. Now, if you will go please. I have work to do."

And with that he closed the door, leaving Anna quite perplexed on the doorstep.

She turned, picked up her rucksack and easel, and set off down the garden path. As she turned to close the gate she was sure she noticed a movement at the window, behind the net curtains. She wondered if it was the foreign man or the old lady.

As she walked down the path towards the Fontaine, she pondered what this was all about. Did this man live in the cottage, or was it the old lady, and he was just visiting? It didn't seem quite right somehow. He didn't seem the type to be visiting old ladies. In fact, she wasn't at all sure about this man. There was something sinister about him. Perhaps it was just his foreign accent, but no, there was something about his eyes too, dark and piercing, as if he could look straight through you.

She reached the clearing on the headland where she

had planned to paint her first picture. Ah yes, this was it, perfect. The sunlight reflecting off the water, and the cliffs glowing red and green against the blue sky. She set up her easel, which was a clever affair with a folding stool you could sit astride and another fold out part to support the painting. Phew, it was a good job she had brought her sun hat. This was going to be quite hot work. She opened her paints, took up her palette and brush and made the first strokes on the paper, but as she did so she was suddenly startled by a picture which had come into her head. Not a picture of the lovely scene before her, nor anything to do with it, but a picture of the man's hand with its stained fingers, and the papers he had been clutching. But they were not papers at all. It was a sea chart that he had been holding, just like the one Tom had.

Anna laughed. I wonder why that came into my head, she said to herself. She thought about it for a while, and then she went back to her painting and, becoming more absorbed in it, she thought no more about the man.

Back at Base Camp 1, Ian was the next to wake up. He looked at his watch, 7.15 am, and then looked over at Tom who was still asleep. Better not wake him just yet, he thought. He admired the bright blue cloth of their new tent, and then he started to plan the day. He wondered what had happened to Bart. No news yet. They couldn't start any proper exploring until Bart arrived, it wouldn't be fair, but in the meantime there was plenty to do. First thing after breakfast they would head off to the tourist office, and he wondered what they would find there. Mrs B seemed certain there would be lots of useful information, but he was not so sure.

After twenty minutes or so Ian was starting to get restless. How on earth could Tom sleep so soundly on these hard mats? He had half a mind to lean over and poke him, but just at that moment Tom stirred, wriggled about, stretched, yawned and opened his eyes.

"About time too," said Ian.

Tom blinked, yawned again and then turned onto his side and slowly propped himself up on his elbow.

"Yeah, what…," he mumbled, "What time is it, Ian?"

"It's nearly 8," said Ian. "Come on, Tom, the girls are probably up by now."

Tom muttered some more, then slowly worked his way into a sitting position. He was not as his best first thing in the morning, but eventually he came to.

"Well I don't know about you, Ian, but I could do with some breakfast," he said.

The boys pulled on some clothes, unzipped the door of the tent and clambered outside. It was a beautiful morning: bright sunshine, a vivid blue sky, not a breath of wind and not a sound to be heard except now and then a bird calling in the surrounding woods. They thought they must have beaten the girls to it as the door of the brown tent was still tightly shut, then they heard shuffling noises and the door was slowly unfastened and a head poked out.

"Where's Anna?" said Shani sleepily.

"Isn't she in there with you?" said Tom.

"Wait a minute," said Ian, spotting the piece of paper pinned to the flagstaff. He unfolded it. "She's left us a note. Gone painting, back 8ish."

"Right, I'd better get dressed," said Shani, disappearing back into the tent.

Five minutes later they were all up and waiting outside for Anna to arrive, as it was now well past 8 am, when who should appear but Mrs B carrying a large cardboard box.

"Ah good, you're all up and about are you? I've brought you some breakfast. Mr Riley thought you might enjoy it camping style, outside in the fresh air, alfresco, as they say."

She started to unpack the contents of the box.

"Toast, butter, marmalade. Sorry if the toast has gone cold. Cornflakes, milk, sugar, bowls, spoons. There, that's the lot. Bon appétit!"

And with that she bustled off again, back toward the hotel.

"Cor! What a great idea of Mr Riley's," said Tom.

"We might as well get started," said Ian. "Anna shouldn't be much longer."

Anna had done as much as she could with her painting. She was really quite pleased with it. It seemed to capture the atmosphere of the place. She unpinned it from the easel and laid it out flat in the sunshine to dry off while she started to pack up.

She had more or less gathered everything together when she heard a cough, then a rustling noise from somewhere just below her. She stood up, and, looking over the top of the gorse bushes in front of her, she saw the man from the cottage making his way along the cliff path. He stopped and looked out to sea. He was holding something in his right hand which he raised to his eye. Then he looked at the papers in his other hand and scribbled some notes. Anna wondered if it was the chart

she had noticed when he opened the door. Luckily, he did not turn around, or he would have seen her. Well, so what if he did, she thought. She had every right to be there. But then she just had the feeling that it would be better if he did not see her, so she ducked down out of sight and waited for him to move on.

Fastening her rucksack, she noticed her phone in the outside pocket and remembered she must try to contact Bart. She looked at her watch. Goodness, 8.30! Was that the time? She had better get back or the others would leave without her.

She picked up her equipment, rose to her full height and looked around for the man. There was no sign of him so she set off at a trot back toward the campsite. It was heavy going, trying to carry her painting gear and run as well, but it was a relief when she arrived back to see that the others were still there.

"Anna! It's going on for 9 o'clock," said Shani. "Everyone's finished breakfast and you haven't even started."

"Yeah... sorry..." said Anna, panting. "Just got to get my breath back..."

Then she told them about the strange man at the cottage and all that had happened to her, whilst trying to eat her breakfast at the same time.

"Have you made contact with Bart?" asked Ian.

"No," said Anna between mouthfuls of cornflakes. "There wasn't time... Just give me a minute to finish these and I'll have another go."

They cleared up the breakfast things, gathered their

rucksacks and made their way to the hotel. Mr and Mrs Riley had gone out for a stroll so they left the cardboard box with Mrs B, thanking her profusely for the wonderful breakfast, and set off for the tourist office.

Anna made a quick call to her mother, to let her know what they were doing, then she sent another text to Bart: "Where are you? The GEESE are waiting."

Chapter 6

Crossing to Big Sark

They followed the road to Big Sark, and before long they arrived at La Coupée, the narrow isthmus that connects Big Sark to Little Sark.

"I don't know if I want to go over that," said Anna, looking down at the sheer drop on both sides and the narrow path across the top.

"It's perfectly ok," Ian assured her. "If a horse and cart and a tractor can get across I'm sure we'll be fine."

"Yeah, but everyone has to get out of the cart to cross the Coupée," said Tom.

"I expect that's in case the horse bolts," said Shani.

"That's right, Shani," said Tom.

They all stepped somewhat gingerly out onto the Coupée and proceeded towards the middle.

"Wow! It certainly is a long way down," said Shani.

Half way across they stopped and admired the view, which was quite spectacular, over Brecqou, Herm, Jethou and Guernsey to the west, and to the east they could make out quite clearly the coast of France. Suddenly, Anna shivered and gripped the railings tightly with both hands.

"Are you alright, Anna?" said Ian.

She had gone quite pale.

"Just one of my funny turns," said Anna. "I'm thinking someone might have fallen off here."

"They would have died, that's for sure," said Tom, looking down at the rocks far below.

"And that's not all," said Anna. "I think this place is haunted. There's something awful that must have happened."

"Come on, Anna," said Shani. "You know you'll only get upset."

Ian put a kindly hand on her shoulder, and she relaxed a little.

"It's okay now," said Tom, trying to reassure her. There might have been a few accidents in the olden days, but, with these railings, there's no reason why anyone should fall over now."

They walked a little further and came to a bronze plaque fixed to a rocky outcrop to one side of the path.

"In 1945 this roadway was rebuilt in concrete and handrails added by German prisoner-of-war labour working under the direction of 259 Field Company Royal Engineers," Ian read out. "There you are, safe as houses, Anna."

Reaching the other side, they continued on their journey.

"Now we're in Big Sark," said Shani.

"Yes, and it does feel different somehow," said Anna.

The road led upwards, past an old stone house on the left, and they trudged along over the brow of the hill and down onto a long straight road leading northward. Some way ahead of them they saw a horse and carriage pull out of a road on the right and turn the same way they were headed.

"Come on," said Tom, setting off at a trot, "Let's catch him up and ask for a lift."

The carriage was trundling along quite slowly and they were able to catch up without too much effort and walk alongside.

"Morning!" said Tom cheerily to the young man driving. "Any chance of a lift to the village?"

"I can give you a taxi ride," replied the driver, "But it will cost you a fiver."

"Oh," said Tom, quite disappointed. "We can't afford that."

He had been excited at the prospect of a carriage ride.

The driver laughed. "Don't be too sad about it. You'll probably get there before us anyway. This horse has only got one speed... dead slow."

He gathered the reins, gave them a shake and commanded the horse: "Come on then! Get a move on!"

The horse broke in a reluctant trot and for a very short while the carriage gathered pace and drew away from them, but, sure enough, just a little way down the road he settled back into a slow amble.

The explorers thought this was quite funny.

"He's right you know," said Ian. "We'll be quicker on foot."

"It would have been a waste of five pounds," said Shani.

Tom was still disappointed.

"Yes, but you can't expect him to do it for nothing," said Ian. "Not if he's doing it for a living."

They waited a while and consulted the map, to make sure they were going in the right direction. Also, they did not want to follow too closely behind the horse and carriage as it would feel less like being on an expedition.

"He must have come up from Dixcart Bay," said Ian, "And this road will take us all the way to the Avenue, as long as we take the right turn before we get to the end."

As soon as the horse and carriage had disappeared

from view they set off again and trudged along a long, dusty road, eventually turning right towards the Avenue. Now and then they were passed by people on bicycles, going this way and that, and all of them saying "Good morning," or "Hello! Lovely day."

"Sark is a very friendly place, isn't it?" said Tom.

"And the people are very polite," said Shani.

They passed the remains of an ancient windmill.

"Look, it's shown on the map," said Tom, "And it has 367 in brackets by it."

"That can't be metres," said Ian. "It must mean 367 feet above sea level. I reckon that's right on top of the island."

"They would have put it on a high spot to catch the wind," said Anna.

Finally they arrived at the spot marked "*i*" on the map, the tourist information centre, which was in an old, stone built cottage. There was a strange looking building attached at the end, with very stout granite walls and a curved stone roof.

"Hey, look. It's the Sark Prison," said Tom. " Isn't it tiny? There must only be room for one or two prisoners, at the most."

"I don't expect they need to use it very often," said Shani. "Not with all the people being so nice and polite."

They trooped into the information centre and were greeted by an elderly lady with grey hair and a kindly smile.

Ian explained that they were seeking more information about the silver mines, Shani mentioned the Sark amethysts and Tom chipped in:

"And anything else to do with the caves, and buried treasure and stuff like that."

"We're explorers you see," said Anna.

"Well, you've come to the right place," said the lady. "We have information sheets on all of those things, but they do cost 15p each. Here they are. You're very welcome to read them, and if you want some copies I can run them off for you."

Anna had already seen a book on Sark folklore and was busily leafing through its pages. There were all sorts of interesting books, pamphlets and maps, some of which were free of charge, and the Islanders spent quite some time choosing the ones they thought might be useful.

"Look at this," said Tom. "There's something called the Sark Hoard, which was found by the windmill we've just seen, in 1718. Some men just dug it up, and it was really, really valuable. Discs and coins from about the first century! Cor, I wonder how that came to be in Sark."

"Well look at this," said Anna. "I'm going to buy this leaflet about Victor Hugo. He was a really famous author, and a painter as well, and he used to come here and stay at the Dixcart Hotel. We saw the signpost for that on the way here."

Eventually they decided which items they wanted to take with them. Shani chose a free Isle of Sark Guide with some lovely photos in it, and Tom and Ian spent some of their pocket money on leaflets about the Sark Hoard and the Silver Mines. They thanked the lady, who had been very kind and helpful, and wandered out into the sunshine, still reading from the books and pamphlets they had acquired.

"See, I told you there was something about the Coupée," said Anna. "Apparently it's haunted by a headless horseman, a floating coffin, a giant dog with flaming red eyes and all sorts of other things. And there was someone blown over the side."

"Yes, but that was before they put the railings up," said Shani.

"To be honest with you," said Tom, "I don't think I'd like to go across it at night."

"Yeah, just imagine that," said Anna. "There are no street lights or anything."

"Okay. What are we going to do next?" said Ian.

"I wouldn't mind a look at the shops in the Avenue," said Shani.

"Me too," said Anna.

They were just finding room for the papers in their rucksacks, and preparing to set off again when the lady from the information centre came rushing out.

"Oh good, you're still here," she said. "Are you the Islanders?"

"How did you know that?" said Tom.

"From the description I've had from this young man I've just been talking to," said the lady. "Someone called Bart? He's on the phone now if you want to speak to him."

Chapter 7

St Malo

Bartholomew Henry was not at all happy. He had been staying with his father and his father's girlfriend, Anne Marie, in the walled town of St Malo. He was not unhappy to be in St Malo. He loved to spend time with his father, and Anne Marie was very kind. He loved St Malo too. He loved to walk along the ramparts surrounding the whole of the old town and admire the beautiful sea views on all sides. The town itself was full of history, heavily fortified in centuries past, its massive walls topped with battlements, towers and gun batteries, and on some of the larger offshore rocks more forts had been built to guard against invaders from the sea.

His father's apartment overlooked the Bassin Vauban* and the Bassin Duguay-Trouin* with boats of all shapes and sizes constantly coming and going through the locks leading out into the estuary of the River Rance and then out to sea.

Bart could see why his father had wanted to move to France. For a seafaring man there could be no better place on earth. There were yachts and pleasure boats, fishing boats, tugs, cargo boats and even the occasional liner, and, best of all in Bart's eyes, the lovely old "Gaffers," as his father called them. The Etoiles: *Molene, Polaire, de France*, the *Fleur du Mai* and, his favourite, *Le Renard**. She was a Corsaire Cutter, about 60 foot long. Her topsides were painted yellow ochre and black, and she even had gun ports and cannons on each side. She was the type of ship favoured in the past by pirates and privateers, being large enough to cope with heavy weather but fast and nimble as well, so that she could out-sail most of her prey. *Le Renard* (the Fox) was a name that suited her very well.

Bart's father had been hired to deliver a new boat from St Malo to Guernsey. The plan was that he and Bart would do this together, and Bart would be dropped off in plenty of time to join up with the rest of the Islanders for the trip to Sark.

Bart had been excited about this for weeks but sadly there had been a delay in completing the boat, and then there had been problems with the ship's papers so that now the Islanders had already left for Sark and Bart was stranded in St Malo. His father was doing his best to hurry things along, and in the meantime he had very kindly arranged for Bart to take a trip around the bay in *Le Renard*. Most of the old gaffers offered excursions and *Le Renard* was probably the most popular.

And so it was that Bart had joined a party of nine others, plus crew, to set sail the previous day. *Le Renard* was moored up in the outer harbour, just outside the lock, and Bart and the other passengers had been ferried out in a rubber dinghy. On reaching the boat they had to climb a rope ladder up over the side. The crew were dressed in old-fashioned clothes and with the backdrop of the ancient walls and buildings it really felt almost like going back in time. The captain issued life-jackets and gave them a brief talk on safety precautions, explaining some matters in broken English for the benefit of Bart and two others.

The crew busied themselves removing the sail covers and preparing the sails for hoisting, then they slipped the mooring ropes and motored out into the estuary. Bart was impressed at how quickly and quietly this was done. He could see that the crew knew exactly what to do and they took great pride in their work. In olden days, of course,

Le Renard would not have had an engine, but it was so quiet you could hardly notice it.

There was a steady breeze blowing and as soon as they had sufficient sea room the captain gave the order to hoist the mainsail. This the crew did, with the aid of various winches, blocks and tackle, singing a sea shanty in French as they hauled together. The mainsail was quickly set and the halyard coiled and neatly tied up on a cleat at the foot of the mast. Bart was amazed at how many ropes there were, and each one for a different purpose.

"Ok, you, you and you!" The first mate pointed at Bart and two others. "Take ziss rope an' when I say 'eave you pull 'ard as you can. Ok … 'eave!"

The crew had prepared the jib and staysail, and, as Bart and the others pulled for all they were worth, the sails were raised in double quick time.

"Whoa!" shouted the mate, "We 'ave a strong crew today, mon capitaine."

The halyards were again neatly coiled and tied off, and now *Le Renard* came alive. She heeled a little but quickly stiffened and surged eagerly forward out into the bay.

"Will you hoist the topsails?" Bart asked the mate.

"No my friend. A leetle too much win'," he replied. "She goes quickly *Le Renard*, n'est ce pas? She like to sail."

Bart nodded in agreement and held onto the guard rail to steady himself as *Le Renard* heeled over some more and picked up speed.

There was hardly time to speak to the other passengers but Bart managed to have a few words with the other

British people onboard, a middle-aged couple from Devon. The man was quite excited about the trip, and obviously enjoying every minute, but his wife seemed a little nervous, clinging on more tightly with every movement of the boat.

Le Renard sailed out towards the island of Cezembre* and then tacked to starboard and sailed in towards the sandy bay of Le Sillon. As she tacked it was all hands to the ropes again, to set the sails for the new course. Some ways off the beach she turned again to starboard and, with the wind behind her, the crew broke out the upper square sail for the remainder of the trip back to the harbour.

Sailing with her old-fashioned rig, amongst the island fortresses guarding the walled town, it seemed again to Bart like going back to olden times. He thought how terrifying it would have been, as an enemy ship, to approach the fearsome defences of St Malo. He wondered if anyone had ever tried it. Then he imagined Le Renard returning victorious to her home port after taking on perhaps a British man-of-war. It was strange to think that, in a way, he was now sailing with the enemy.

All too soon they arrived back in port and it was time to disembark. It was at this moment that disaster struck. It had certainly felt like a disaster to Bart at any rate. He was climbing over the side and down into the dinghy when his fleece caught on a piece of rigging. It jerked free but unfortunately the pocket where he kept his mobile phone was unzipped, and somehow the phone was catapulted out of his pocket and into the sea. It seemed to happen in slow motion. Bart was able to watch it floating in a graceful arc through the air, then … plop. In it went.

"Oh la la!" exclaimed one of the French ladies.

In fact everyone who had seen the incident was suitably shocked and sorry for Bart. This was something of a comfort, but he was still very upset about it. What would his mother say? Worse than that, how on earth could he contact the other Islanders? He had not written down Anna's phone number and he could not remember it. They would be leaving for Sark, and he did not even know the name of the hotel where they were staying. He had expected to be able to make all of the arrangements on his mobile.

"Pauvre Bart," said Anne Marie, giving him a hug, when he arrived back at the apartment. "Don't worry. Your father will be here soon. He will know what to do."

But Bart was still feeling wretched and he went up to his room. He needed some peace and quiet, and the view from his window of the boats and the constant flow and low babble of people walking the ramparts helped to take his mind off things. After a while he started to feel better. Some time later he heard the telephone ring, and then he heard footsteps on the stairs as Anne Marie came up and knocked on his door.

"Good news, Bart," she said. "The boat is here, but now your father will be late. He hopes to sail tomorrow but there is much to do."

Anne Marie could see that Bart was still upset about losing his phone. "Pauvre garçon!" she said. "Viens. You come with me. We go buy ice-creams."

Bart's father did not arrive home till late that evening,

by which time there was no point in trying to contact anyone.

"Don't worry, Bart," said his father. "These things happen. I'll phone your mother in the morning, and I'm sure we'll be able to contact the others some how. Leave it to me."

The next day Bart's mother had taken the news better than he had expected.

"I don't mind the phone going overboard," she said to Bart's father. "You just make sure it doesn't happen to Bart."

Bart and his father decided that the best place to phone might be the Sark tourist office, so they contacted Bart's grandmother in Guernsey and she looked up the number in her telephone book.

"I know it's a bit of a long shot," said Bart's father to the lady who answered the phone, "But we wondered if you might know where they are staying and how we can contact them. Look, I'll hand you over to my son, Bart, and he can give you more information."

Bart provided the names of Mr and Mrs Riley, and then described the Islanders.

"Two girls... one fair and one dark," said the Sark lady, "And two boys from Guernsey... one tall... Do you know? You're not going to believe this, but they've just this minute been here in the office! Hold the line, will you, and I'll dash out and see if I can catch them."

Chapter 8

Bob the Boatman

"Bart!" said Anna. "Where are you? Why haven't you phoned? We've been worried about you."

Bart explained what had happened. "We were hoping to sail over today," he said, "But we still don't have clearance from Customs, and it's getting too late now."

"Oh dear. That's a shame about your phone," said Anna, "But we've not done any proper exploring yet. We'll wait till you arrive."

"No. You'd better get on," said Bart. "At this rate it will be time to leave by the time I get there."

"Okay. Well I hope we'll see you tomorrow then," said Anna. "Port Gorey you said? About 3pm if all goes well. Okay. Have a nice trip and see you soon."

Anna told the others what Bart had said.

"It's a shame about his phone," said Tom. "We could have used the two phones like walky talkies. I bet he had a great time on that pirate ship though."

"I think Bart is right," said Ian. "We'd better get on with our exploring or there won't be enough time to do the whole island."

"Poor Bart," said Shani. "He must be wishing like mad he was here with us.

They spent the next half hour or so strolling along the Avenue looking at the shops. At frequent intervals the girls would disappear inside for a closer look at something which had caught their eye, while the boys waited outside. They passed a café.

"I don't know about you, Ian," said Tom, "But I could really do with something to eat."

Ian looked at his watch. "It's only half past ten, Tom."

"Well there you are then," said Tom. "Nearly time for elevenses."

In the last shop, the girls were in there such a long time that Ian and Tom had to go in and fetch them out.

Eventually they reached the end of the Avenue, and the top of Harbour Hill, where two carriages were parked, waiting for customers to arrive from the boat. The two drivers were talking to each other in Sark patois.

"Can you understand what they're saying?" Shani whispered to Tom.

"Some of it I can," said Tom, "But I don't know much patois, and it's different from the one from the Vale."

"Somebody told me it's like old Norman French," said Ian.

"So they would sound to us like people speaking in old English?" said Anna. "That's really funny. Imagine passing someone in the street, and they're speaking in old English."

They stopped by a path leading to a cycle hire shop.

"Cor, if we could use bikes we could get around much quicker," said Tom.

"Yeah, but it's too expensive," said Ian.

"And it wouldn't be proper exploring anyway," said Anna.

"Look over here!" Shani called out.

She had wandered down a side road and found a gateway in the hedge.

"Look, there's a sign for Dixcart Bay, and a path. I think it's a path anyway, although it's a little overgrown."

"Mrs B's cousin lives somewhere around there," said Ian. "Let's have a look at the map."

They gathered around the map and tried to find the path.

"It could be this one here," said Ian. "It goes down through Baker's Valley, and then we might be able to connect up with that other path leading to the Hog's Back."

"It's no good," said Tom, taking off his rucksack, "I'm famished. I'm going to have a sandwich before we go any further."

So they sat on a low stone wall by the roadside and drank from their water bottles while Tom ate his sandwich and passed around some digestive biscuits which he had brought along.

"Might as well eat these before they get too badly broken," he said. "That's the only trouble with digestives."

After Tom had been refuelled they gathered their things, filed through the narrow gateway, and set off towards Dixcart.

The path led them down through a wooded valley where there was no one to be seen except themselves. As they went deeper into the valley the path became harder to follow and they were not quite sure if they were heading in the right direction. They had to scramble up and down over tree roots and through the undergrowth and they started to think that perhaps they had lost their way. Then, after many twists and turns, they came to a crossroads where a wider track, which showed more signs of regular use, led up out of the woods and over the brow of a hill to their left.

"This must be it," said Ian, consulting the map. "I reckon the house must be just over the top of that hill."

"Yes, but how could anybody live there?" said Shani. "You can hardly get to it except on foot."

"Let's go and see," said Anna. "That's where Mrs B has marked it on the map."

They trudged up the hill, the path leading them out from the shade of the trees into the warm sunshine, through a wide sweep of bracken, and then, as they reached the brow of the hill, they could see the sea. The path continued down into another copse where it turned sharply to the right and led them into a clearing with a raised earth bank at the far end, topped with bushes, amongst which there was a man lying down spying with binoculars at something on the other side. The man must have heard them because he turned and gestured to them to get down while he wriggled backwards down from the bank.

"Keep down!" he mouthed out to them in a loud whisper. "I don't want them to know I'm watching them!"

Then, still in a crouching position, he beckoned them to follow him through a path leading down into what looked like an old quarry, where a tiny little cottage with

a red painted tin roof stood to one side.

"Sorry about that," said the man. "You must be the Islanders. I've been expecting you."

He spoke with a thick Sark accent. He was small and wiry with grey hair and black bushy eyebrows which shielded a pair of twinkling blue eyes.

"It's old Frenchy out there. You must have seen them, in that black boat. Turned up yesterday. I don't know what they're up to, but if I catch them fishing in our waters they'll be for it."

"We did see a French boat in that little cove down by the silver mines," said Ian.

"Port Gorey," it's called," said Anna. "That's where we're going to meet Bart tomorrow."

"Was she an old black fishing boat?" asked the man.

"Yes, she was," said Tom. "We watched them lower their dinghy over the side and row in."

"Did you now? Well I'll tell you what. You can give me a hand if you like. Just to keep an eye on them. We don't mind French yachts visiting, that's perfectly fine, but a fishing boat lurking about the place, well I think they've got a bit of a nerve if you ask me.

Anyway, what is it I can do for you? Something about a map was it, or a sea chart? Come inside and make yourselves comfortable. Now which of you is which? You may as well call me Bob. Most people do."

He opened the door and ushered them into the cottage, which was tiny and basic but very homely inside. The main room had a cooking range, an old Belfast sink with a wooden draining board and a few cupboards. There was a table and four chairs and a daybed with cushions against the wall to make a sofa.

Tom produced his chart and Bob unfolded it and spread it out on the table.

"Aha … mmm … I see," he said, examining the lines and figures very carefully. Then he stood up, thought for a moment and muttered under his breath as if doing calculations in his head. He picked up a notebook and pencil and started to scribble down figures of his own. The Islanders looked at one another expectantly but said nothing.

"Mmm …" said Bob eventually. "I don't know what you've got here at all. Now wait a minute though. This chart must be … let's have a look … yes, it's dated 1979. And these lines here, they look like a three point fix. See there's a transit there: Point Banquette and Point Robert Lighthouse, and another one there: La Conchée on Point Chateau. Now, that gives your position there."

He stabbed the chart with his finger, but the others did not quite understand what he was saying.

"And all of these figures here."

He moved his finger to the scribbled figures in columns in the bottom right hand corner of the chart.

"That's where he's converted the compass readings from magnetic to true. Variation of about seven degrees at that time, whereas it's only about two degrees now, if you follow me?"

He looked around at them, and could see they had not really understood.

"It's a pity Bart isn't here," said Tom. "He's very good

at this sort of thing."

"Well, I'll try and explain," said Bob. "Imagine if you're out fishing on your boat, and say you just found a really good spot and you're hauling them in like mad. Well naturally, you want to mark it on your chart so you know exactly where it is and you can come back to it another day. You get the idea?"

The Islanders nodded.

"So you look around, and you can see two things which line up. Like on the chart, see … the lighthouse and the point behind it. So you draw a line on the chart and you know you must be somewhere on that line. But then you need another line to cross over it to show exactly where you are, so you look to the right and the left and then you can see that this rock, the Conchée, is directly below the point. So you line that up with your ruler and draw another line. And Bingo! The two lines cross over here, and that's where you are. But if you want to make absolutely sure you need a third line, and that's what he's done here by using his hand bearing compass."

"Do you mean one like this?" said Tom, fishing out the compass from his rucksack.

"Yes, that's right," said Bob.

Taking the compass from Tom, he put it up to his eye and scanned around the room as if searching for something on which to take a bearing.

"See, in this case they took a bearing on L'Etac, and after converting it to true. Hmm … I can see I've lost you again. Well take it from me, you must only ever draw true bearings on a chart, and that's what he's done here. You can see they all cross over here, and that's where you are. You can mark it on your chart and come back for more fish any time you like."

"I wonder if that man on the cliffs was taking bearings," said Anna. "It could have been a compass he was using."

"So do you think it was a fisherman who made those marks on the chart?" asked Shani.

"No, my dear," said Bob. "You wouldn't catch many fish there. Maybe he just wanted to check his position."

"But what if it was something else?" said Tom. "Could there be a wreck down there? Maybe it was a diver who meant to come back for a treasure chest full of gold and precious jewels, but he never did and maybe it's still there!"

"Well, it could be, Tom" said Bob. "There have been many ships come to grief around the coast of Sark, and some of them with treasure too of one sort or another, but in that particular spot there's plenty of water so I would have thought it fairly unlikely. But it is possible."

Tom nodded, pleased that there was still some hope of finding treasure.

"Can you explain to us," said Ian, "About converting the compass bearings?"

"Oh no," said Anna. "It's giving me a headache."

We'll leave it for another time," said Bob. "Tell me about this man on the cliffs. You reckon he was taking bearings?"

"He might have been," said Anna. "He didn't seem very nice to me. And I'm worried he might have done something to the old lady."

"Old lady?" said Bob.

"Yes, we saw this old lady who looked like a witch," said Shani. "She was sweeping with her broom outside a tiny little white cottage on the cliffs by the Fontaine."

"Oh," said Bob with a laugh. "You mean old Agnes? She's no witch, she's a sweet old thing, wouldn't hurt a fly."

"When I went there this morning," said Anna, "She wasn't there. It was this spooky sort of foreign man who answered the door."

"I shouldn't worry about that," said Bob. "She has been known to take in guests over the summer. Sometimes the tourist office send people down to her if they've nowhere else available. Come to think of it, I did hear that two men, from Holland I think it was, turned up out of the blue the other day. Or was it Belgium? Birdwatchers apparently. Maybe it was one of them."

"He didn't seem like a birdwatcher to me," said Anna. "If he was birdwatching why would he have a sea chart like Tom's, and why did he answer the door and not the old lady?"

"Well I must say I'm impressed by your powers of observation," said Bob. "They told me you were a clever lot, you Islanders. I'd like you to help me if you can, while you're over here, just to keep an eye on that French boat, and maybe those birdwatchers too. If you see anything suspicious you just let me know. I'll write down my phone number for you. But I wouldn't worry about old Agnes. She was probably out back when you called, or busy doing something or other.

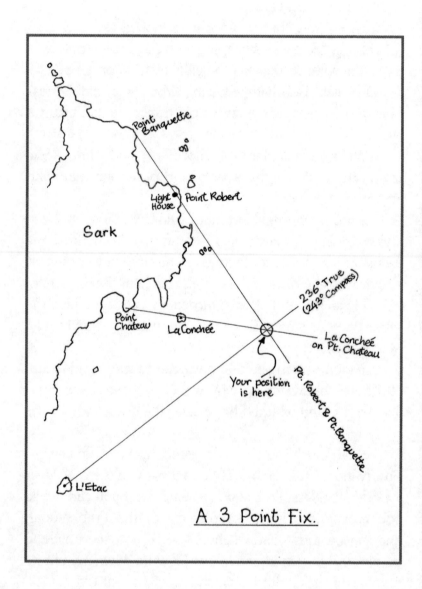

Point Banquette

Light House ● Point Robert

Sark

Point Chateau

La Conchée

236° True (243° Compass)

La Conchée on Pt. Chateau

Your position is here

Pt. Robert & Pt. Banquette

L'Etac

A 3 Point Fix.

Now I don't mean to be rude but it's way past my lunch hour. Have you kids had anything to eat?"

"No we haven't," said Tom.

"We've brought packed lunches though, so you don't have to worry about us," said Ian.

"Well if you don't mind I'll get myself something to eat, and you're welcome to have lunch here with me if you like."

"Great," said Tom. "Do you mind if we start? I'm absolutely starving."

Chapter 9

The Birdwatchers and
the Black Boat

Over lunch the Islanders asked Bob about his work and about his duties as a special constable.

"I expect you have all sorts of people coming on the boat trips," said Ian.

"I certainly do," said Bob. "Do you know I had one chap last year with his hand and his arm all bandaged up, right up to his elbow. What on earth have you done to yourself I said. Turned out he was a geologist, one of these folks who go around with a hammer, chipping away at the stones. He was mad for them apparently and he reckoned Sark was just the place for it. Anyway, there he was at Grande Grève chipping away at the cliff and this big piece of rock falls off and bashes his hand. So that put a stop to it. He had to go to the doctor. I said to him: Sark has got a way of getting her own back!"

Ian felt slightly uncomfortable at hearing this because he had secretly been hoping to find some interesting rock samples himself. He wondered how Sark would feel about it if he took a few pieces home.

"That tiny little prison by the tourist office," said Anna. "Is it still in use?"

"Oh yes," said Bob. "It's all ready to use if we need it. Not that we use it often mind. Only very occasionally, if someone has a few drinks too many and gets a bit uppity or something like that. Then we might have to put them in there to cool off for a while."

After lunch they decided to head back towards Little Sark via Dixcart Bay. Bob led them to a path and gave them directions. "Just turn left at the end and it'll take you straight to the bay," he said. "Going swimming are you? It's a lovely day for it."

They made their way down a narrow, winding path, which looked as if it was seldom used. Now and then the tall bushes on both sides arched over the top, making a leafy tunnel. Then they came to a spot high above the bay where the undergrowth suddenly petered out and they had a perfect view out to sea.

"Look, it's that black boat," said Tom, "And she's moored almost exactly where those lines cross on my chart. I bet there is treasure there, and they're probably diving down and grabbing it right now."

Ian took his telescope and trained it on the boat.

"It doesn't look like it, Tom. There's nobody on board at all. No, wait a minute…Yes, there they are. Look, there's three of them in that rubber dinghy, close in to shore.

"Oh yes," said Anna. "I can see them. Do you think they're coming in to the beach?"

"No, they're just pottering along, close in to the cliffs. No, I've lost them now. They've gone around the corner."

The Islanders continued on their way down and joined the main path leading to the bay.

"Oh blow it!" said Tom, as they approached the end of the path, "There's people on the beach. We can't do our yahoos."

"Yahoo!" said Shani softly. "We'll just do it quietly, Tom."

"It's not the same quietly," said Tom wistfully.

"Oh no," said Anna. "It's that weirdo from Cliff Cottage. And that must be his friend."

"Oh yes," said Shani. "The two birdwatchers."

The birdwatchers were sitting at the top of the pebble beach, eating sandwiches and looking out to sea. They turned and nodded to the Islanders as they walked past, then hurriedly started to pack their things away and leave.

"There's something odd going on here," said Anna. "Don't you think it's odd that we should come across the two lots of people that Bob asked us to watch out for on the same beach at the same time?"

"They could have had a secret meeting on the beach," said Shani, "Just before we arrived."

"Yes," said Tom, "And the black boaters were actually on their way back."

"Could be," said Ian, looking around the beach, "But there are some people over there, and a couple down there by those rocks, so it wouldn't have been that secret.

Anyway, now we're here, what are we going to do. I fancy having a look at that hole in the rock over there."

"Can we go for a swim first?" said Tom.

"A nice refreshing swim would be just the thing after all of our trekking," said Shani.

"Okay," said Ian and Anna.

"Come on then," said Tom, "Last one in's a sissy!"

They quickly changed into their bathers and hobbled down over the pebbles.

"Hold on a minute. What's this?" said Shani.

She had caught a glimpse of something in amongst the pebbles. She reached down, picked up a tiny vivid green stone, and held it to the light.

"Isn't it pretty?" she said. "Do you think it's an emerald?"

The others crowded around.

"It's probably a piece of glass," said Ian, "Worn smooth by the action of the waves."

"It is pretty though," said Anna.

"Let's see if we can find some more," said Tom.

"I've found one already," said Ian, holding up another tiny stone. "This one's white. Must be a diamond!"

"I've found another green one!" said Anna, holding up her prize.

After a few minutes of searching they had collected enough stones so that each of them had one diamond and one emerald, and they saved two for Bart as well.

"Something tells me they can't really be precious gems," said Ian. "Not if they're so easy to find."

"Well they are precious to me," said Shani. "Even if

they are only glass, I will treasure them always, and I will keep them with my bullet* and my ormer shell from last year."

Tom smiled at Shani. Sometimes she could be really sweet, he thought.

"Come on then, what about that swim," said Anna.

Shani took the emeralds and diamonds up to where they had left their clothes, for safekeeping, before she joined the others.

"Come on in," shouted Tom. "The water's lovely."

"No it isn't," shouted Anna. "Don't listen to him, Shani. It's freezing!"

"Come on in, or we'll come over and splash you," called Tom, as Shani gamely waded in up to her knees.

Tom was further out, treading water. "Here, watch this," he said, and did a somersault. He came up spluttering. "Hey, what do you think of that! Come on, Ian. Race you to those rocks over there."

The girls left the boys to it and had a leisurely paddle in the shallows.

After half an hour or so they all hobbled back up the beach to dry themselves off.

"Cor, that was nice," said Tom. "I feel better after that."

They changed back into their clothes and went over to inspect the hole in the rock which had caught Ian's eye. Anna took her sketch pad. "I've seen this in quite a few pictures at the tourist office," she said. "It would make a lovely painting."

The hole was quite big enough for all of them to walk

through together. "Isn't it amazing what nature can do," said Ian.

Anna finished off a quick sketch of the hole in the rock and then they thought, as time was pressing on, they had better start on their way back.

"I'll just phone mother," said Anna, "So she knows we're okay."

She explained to her mother where they were and assured her they were on their way back and would meet her at the hotel in about an hour.

The path leading up from Dixcart was steep, and hard work to climb, but it was so peaceful and the views along the cliffs leading towards Little Sark were stunning; a series of headlands in dusty shades of green and brown, receding into the distance, overlapping one behind the other, falling steeply into a grey and silver sea.

All along the path they kept an eye on the black boat. The men in the rubber dinghy had returned to it and the boat was motoring very slowly, close inshore, towards Little Sark.

They were approaching La Coupée when Anna suddenly spotted two people crossing over. "Quick. Get down everyone," she said. "I reckon it's those two birdwatchers again. We don't want them to see us."

They all crouched down and made their way under cover, as silently as they could, towards a high ridge looking down over La Coupée.

"Have a look with your telescope, Ian," said Anna. "But don't let them see you."

The others kept their heads down as Ian wriggled flat

on his stomach to the edge of the ridge and spied on the birdwatchers. After a minute he wriggled back down again.

"It is them," he whispered, "And the black boat is down there too, close in to the Coupée, just below us but you can't quite see her from here."

"That's the second time today we've come across the boat and the birdwatchers in the same place, at the same time," said Shani.

"I reckon they're up to something," said Tom. "They could be sending each other secret signals."

"It didn't look like it," said Ian. "One of them was leaning on the railings, looking over towards Guernsey, and the other one was having a smoke."

"Yes, but they weren't birdwatching were they?" said Anna.

From way below they heard the sound of the black boat's engine being powered up, then she drove out of the bay and continued on her way around Little Sark, but at greater speed.

Ian crept back up to the ridge and looked for the birdwatchers. "It's okay," he said, wriggling back down. "They're leaving, nearly over on the other side. We'll be able to cross over in a minute, without them seeing us."

"Well that's strange isn't it?" said Anna. "The black boat appears, the birdwatchers appear. The black boat leaves, the birdwatchers leave."

They waited a few minutes, to make sure that the birdwatchers would be well ahead of them on the road, then they crossed over and made their way back to La

Sablonnerie.

"Ah, there you all are," Mr Riley greeted them. "I'm sorry to tell you we've had a telephone message from Bart's father. They won't be able to make it here tomorrow."

"Oh no," said Anna and Shani together.

"I'm afraid so," said Mr Riley. "More delays with the paperwork unfortunately."

"Poor Bart," said Tom. "He must be going mental."

"It is a shame isn't it? The French can be absolute sticklers over paperwork," said Mr Riley, "But there is some good news. His father is sorting out a replacement phone, so Bart should be able to contact you soon and fill you in with the details."

"But when will he get here?" asked Anna.

"Probably the day after tomorrow, I should think," said Mr Riley.

The Islanders were back at Base Camp 1, changing for dinner, when Anna's phone bleeped.

"I've had a text!" she called out, and, quickly as they could, they all gathered outside to hear Bart's message, which Anna read out to them.

"So sorry. Completely fed up. Stuck here till Tuesday. So bored I'm reading French newspapers. Anything happening there? X."

"Poor old Bart," said Ian. "He's really missing out, isn't he?"

"Yeah, we're all having a really great time and he's got nothing to do except try and read in French. How awful is that?" said Tom.

"Shall we tell him about the black boat and the

birdwatchers and everything?" said Shani.

"I think that might make it worse," said Anna, starting to text back. "I'll just say ... Nothing much happening yet ... See you Tuesday ... love from all. Xx."

That night at dinner Anna kicked out under the table at Tom and Ian. "It's them," she hissed, indicating wildly with her eyes as two men entered the restaurant and made their way to a table in the middle of the room. "It's the birdwatchers. Don't turn around."

Ian and Tom would have had to turn around completely to see the men, as their table was directly behind them.

"Anna, what are you up to?" said Anna's mother sternly. "Do please try to behave yourself."

"Sorry, mother," she shrugged, then whispered at the boys. "Try and get a peek one at a time, but don't make it too obvious. I'll keep an eye from this side but see if you can hear what they're saying."

"Anna, can we be involved in this conversation please," said Mrs Riley.

"Sorry, mother," said Anna, with a cough. "I was just clearing my throat."

The others could see there was no way Mrs Riley believed this, but she was used to being exasperated by her daughter. She just sighed, and continued with her meal.

Mr Riley started exuberantly telling them about his day, where he had been, what he had seen and the people he had met on his travels.

"First we tried to find that Venus Pool," he said, "But do you think we could find it? No, not a bit of it. I'm half thinking it might be a joke that the Sarkees have with the visitors. You know, like sending them on a wild goose chase. There were a couple of signs leading us to the edge of the cliffs, then there was nothing. Well, I had a jolly good scramble over the rocks, didn't I dear? And I found a few rock pools. I don't know if one of them was the Venus Pool or not..."

While Mr Riley was chatting, Anna and Shani were watching the two birdwatchers. They both had a foreign look about them, and, now and then, Anna could hear them talking to the waiter, as they ordered food and drinks. Yes, it could be a Dutch accent, Anna thought to herself. Maybe Bob was right. They seemed fairly quiet and normal really. Perhaps they were birdwatchers after all, just two ordinary men on holiday.

Ian and Tom had sneaked a quick look at the two men, just to make sure they would recognise them again. There was nothing really of particular note. Dressed in dark trousers and sports jackets, they both had dark hair, one going thin on top, and the other one left the table twice during the meal. Probably going out for a cigarette, thought Tom. They could hear the men talking from time to time, but it was in a foreign language which neither Tom nor Ian could understand.

"Anyway," said Mr Riley, "The woman in the shop said she reckoned there was never any such thing as Sarkstone, and it was brought over from Bulgaria or some such place, but I'm not sure if that's right. I was chatting to one of the tractor men on the farm and he reckoned they did used to mine for Sarkstone, and he said they sometimes dig some up when they're ploughing the fields. I don't know what to make of it really. It's something of a mystery."

By this time they had finished their puddings. Tom thought his had been particularly delicious. It looked as if the birdwatchers had finished their meal too.

"Can I get you anything else?" the waiter asked them, "More coffee, perhaps a glass of sloe gin?"

"No thank you," one of them answered. "We have to be rising early in the morning."

They paid the bill and made their way out of the restaurant. As they passed the Islanders the man whom Anna had met at Cliff Cottage nodded at her but said nothing.

"Blast," said Anna quietly to the others. "They've spotted us."

Back at Base Camp the Islanders were at last able to talk about the two men.

"I think we should definitely keep an eye on them," said Ian, "But they didn't seem that bad to me."

"They were talking very quietly though," said Tom. "As if they didn't want anyone to hear what they were saying, even though we couldn't understand it anyway."

"They seemed quite ordinary to me," said Shani. "Surely if they were criminals, if they had something to hide, they wouldn't be out and about in restaurants. They'd be more likely keeping out of sight."

"Yes, I know they look fairly ordinary," said Anna, "But there's something about them, especially the one I first met at the old lady's cottage, the one who nodded at me tonight, I just don't like the look of him. It's almost as if he knows we're watching him, and he's playing a game with us. And when I first met him he really was very abrupt, and you should have seen the look in his eye."

"Well, Bob said we should keep an eye on them, so I suppose we should carry on doing that," said Ian. "They said they were getting up early in the morning. Maybe we should too."

Chapter 10

Caught Out

The next morning ran true to form. Ian and Anna woke up early whilst the other two continued to sleep soundly in their beds. Ian looked at his watch. 6.15 am. He knew it would take ages to wake Tom so he decided to get dressed and sneak off without him. He wanted to see what the birdwatchers were up to. As quietly as possible he slowly unzipped the door of the tent, crept outside, and then zipped it up again. As he did this he heard a noise behind him. He turned to see Anna already up and dressed and carrying her painting equipment. She silently put a finger to her lips and gestured to him to follow her. As soon as they were out of earshot they were able to speak.

"Best not wake up the sleeping beauties," said Anna.

Ian laughed. "Not much chance of that with Tom," he said. "You'd never wake him up at this time of day. Are you going out painting?"

"Looks like it, doesn't it?" said Anna, "But that's my cunning plan. I thought it might be interesting to see why the birdwatchers had to be up early, and if they see me I'll pretend I'm painting."

"Good idea," said Ian. "I wanted to do that too but I don't suppose both of us can pretend to be painting?"

"Don't see why not," said Anna. "Here you can help carry my stuff."

She handed the easel over to Ian and they continued on their way towards Cliff Cottage. The weather was not quite so nice as the previous day. It was overcast, but dry and not too chilly.

Ten minutes later they had reached Cliff Cottage. They found a suitable hiding place, amongst the gorse, from which they could see the front porch. Just as there had been the previous day there was a curl of white smoke from the chimney.

"Probably still having their breakfast," whispered Ian.

Anna nodded.

They waited for five minutes, then five minutes more. Ian looked at his watch. It seemed like ages but nothing happened.

"I wonder if they're out already," whispered Anna. "We might have missed them."

Suddenly, they nearly jumped out of their skins as a loud voice boomed out at them.

"What is the meaning of this?"

Out of nowhere the two birdwatchers had suddenly appeared and were glowering down at them from a raised bank just behind their hiding place.

Anna and Ian were speechless.

"So, you have nothing to say?" said the thin one. "Then

you had better go or you will be in big trouble."

"We will not have this spying," said the other one, "This foolish behaviour. You will go right now, and you will keep away from us. You understand?"

Ian and Anna had both gone bright red. They nodded and tried to apologise.

"We're sorry if —"

"We are not interested in what you have to say," said the larger man. He shook his walking stick at them. "You go now. And don't come back."

Ian and Anna hurriedly gathered their things and ran off back towards Base Camp.

As they reached the brow of the hill, they heard the sound of a marine engine. They turned and, looking out to sea, they saw the black boat heading away from Little Sark towards Herm and Jethou.

They looked at one another wide eyed, but didn't know what to say.

They looked over toward Cliff Cottage, but there was no sign of the birdwatchers.

"Crikey! That was a bit of a shock," said Ian eventually.

They waited a while and caught their breath.

"I'm so sorry, Ian. I hope I haven't got us into trouble," said Anna.

"No, I'm just as much to blame," said Ian.

They waited a while longer and watched as the black boat drew further and further away from Little Sark.

"Hang on a minute though," said Anna. "That's only the third time we've caught them hanging around the black boat. That's why they were so angry, Ian, because we caught them at it. There must be some kind of connection between them."

"Maybe. But I think it was them who caught us out," said Ian. "Maybe we should just keep away from them, like they said."

"No, Ian," said Anna. "Don't you see? That's just what

they want us to do. They don't want us watching them because they have something to hide."

"Hmm, well okay," said Ian, "But we're going to have to be really careful they don't see us. I don't want to be caught out like that again."

By the time they arrived back at Base Camp, Tom and Shani were awake and they were able to tell them what had happened.

"Oh no," said Shani, "How embarrassing!"

"The black boat again?" said Tom. "I'm sure you're right, Anna. I bet they're working together, and I reckon they're up to something dodgy too. I vote we carry on watching them."

"That's all very well for you to say, Tom," said Ian, "But you didn't get caught like we did. They don't strike me as the sort of people you can mess around with."

"Ian's right," said Anna. "We will have to be really careful."

"Yes, but if the black boat has gone there will be nothing much to spy on today," said Shani. What are we going to do?"

"We would have been going to meet Bart," said Anna.

"Well, as we're not, how about going to see Mr Mahy's friend? I've got his name and address," said Tom.

Just at that moment Mrs B appeared with the cardboard box containing their breakfast.

"Good morning, campers," she said, "And how are we all today?"

"Very well, thank you," they chorused.

~ *Islanders Adventures in Sark* ~

Tom had fished out the piece of paper with the address of Mr Mahy's friend on it.

"Do you know where this is Mrs B?" he asked.

"Oh yes, that's easy," said Mrs B. "Peter Hamon, Donkey Lane. Yes, I know Mr Hamon. It's just the other side of the Coupée. Walk along the main road and you'll see a sign for the Dos D'Ane* on your left. Then you take the next left and there's a row of cottages. I think his is the third one along."

"Thank you Mrs B," said the Islanders.

"No problem. Everything else okay? Anything else you need? Well I'll be off then. Bon appétit!" And with that she whizzed off back along the path to the hotel.

The Islanders ate a hearty breakfast, then drifted up to the hotel to wash and meet up with Mr and Mrs Riley.

"Good morning, you lot," said Mr Riley. "Pity about the weather isn't it?" He squinted up into the clouds. "I think it might clear up later though. So, any plans for today? We're off to the Seigneurie gardens. Would you like to come along?"

The Islanders thanked him politely, but explained that they wanted to leave the serious exploring until Bart arrived, and that Tom needed to call in on Mr Hamon.

"Oh yes, such a shame about Bart," said Mr Riley. "Mind you, that only leaves four days to explore the whole island. You'll have to get your skates on."

While the rest of the Islanders filled their water bottles and set about arranging provisions for the day, Anna set up her easel and made a rough watercolour sketch of La Sablonnerie. Tom made the last of his loaf of bread into

~ *106* ~

sandwiches, some corned beef and some cheese, and Mrs B provided them with fruit and slices of sponge cake for afters.

It was a relaxed start to the day and, in a way, they were relieved that they would not have to worry about the black boat, nor the birdwatchers, especially Anna and Ian, after having been caught and shouted at.

They strolled along the lane leading to La Coupée, enjoying the fresh air and the scenery. Mr Riley had been right about the weather. There was blue sky now appearing amongst the clouds with the sun shining through in places dancing on the sea and turning it from grey to blue. On reaching La Coupée, Tom noticed another inscription on the right hand side. "224 Works Section KE. 1945," he read out. "Do you think that's King's Engineers?" he said.

"Probably," said Ian. "That would tie up with the one we saw yesterday."

They stopped to admire the view half way over, then continued on their way towards the Dos D'Ane. There was no sign of the birdwatchers, nor of the black boat. They soon reached the sign for the Dos D'Ane and, further on, they found the lane leading to a row of cottages, two of whitewashed stone and the third of black weather boarding with a red tin roof. From inside came the sound of a kettle whistling on a stove.

"Good. He must be in," said Tom. He knocked on the door and a dog started barking. The whistling of the kettle stopped and the door was opened by a girl, roughly of their own age, perhaps a year older. She had medium length dark brown hair and pale grey eyes, and she was struggling to hold back a very boisterous black and white collie dog.

"Be quiet, Ben," she said. "Oh, I am sorry about that," as the dog struggled free and leapt up joyously at Tom.

"Don't worry," said Tom. "We love dogs, don't we Ian?"

Ian and Shani nodded in agreement. It was only Anna who wasn't sure.

"Okay then, I'll let him go if you don't mind. He's very friendly really. It's only small children he doesn't like."

Ben lolloped around amongst the Islanders, wagging his tail, panting, beaming up at them and generally welcoming them like long lost friends.

"Come on, Ben. That's enough now," said the girl. "Oh dear, he's such a character. Anyway, what can I do for you?"

"We're looking for Mr Peter Hamon," said Tom. "We're over from Guernsey, and a friend of his asked us to call on him."

"That's my grandpa," said the girl. "Come on in and I'll go and fetch him for you."

The Islanders and their new friend Ben crowded into the front room while the girl disappeared through an inner door and returned shortly with an elderly gentleman on her arm. He was clearly somewhat frail and walked slowly with the aid of a stick.

"What's all this racket going on?" he said. "My goodness me!"

"These people are from Guernsey," said the girl in a

loud voice. "They know a friend of yours in Guernsey."

Obviously, the poor old chap was deaf as well, thought Tom. I'd better speak up. "Mr Mahy? From L'Islet?" said Tom.

"Mahy? Which Mahy?" said Mr Hamon. He spoke in a thick Sark accent.

"Bert Mahy," said Tom, feeling a little uncomfortable as he never usually referred to Mr Mahy as 'Bert.' "You used to go fishing with him, and shooting rabbits."

Mr Hamon thought for a moment. "Oh, Bert Mahy," he said. "Yes, of course. So you know Bert Mahy do you? Ah yes, he's a very old friend of mine, you know, since we were young lads. Boy, we used to have some fun in those days. I could tell you some stories. Here, put the kettle on, Kaz. Let's have a cup of tea."

Kaz made cups of tea and passed around the biscuits while Mr Hamon entertained the Islanders with tales of bygone days.

"My father used to keep some cows in those days," said Mr Hamon, "And we used to make cream and butter, and Bert wanted to make some butter too. So my sister gave him a jam jar and some milk and said 'You just keep shaking it, Bert, and eventually you'll have some butter.' So he spent ages, Bert, shaking this jar, and eventually he makes this tiny pat of butter. Cor, he was so proud of it though. 'Good,' he says. 'I'm going to take this butter home for my tea tomorrow.' Because he was leaving the next day, you see. Anyway, he goes out and leaves it on the table, and my sister and me, we were very naughty in those days, well, we takes the butter and hides it in the cupboard.

Anyway, Bert comes back. 'Where's my butter?' he says.

'The dog must have eaten it,' says my sister."

Mr Hamon shook with laughter at this point. "You should have seen his face!" he said.

The Islanders could see the funny side too, and even Kaz, who seemed quite serious most of the time, smiled and patted her grandfather on the shoulder.

"But did Mr Mahy not have any butter to take home?" said Anna.

Mr Hamon smiled at her. "Of course he did, my dear. My mother sent him home with his little pat of butter, and a big pat of butter, and some cream, and some eggs too."

"Mr Mahy said you used to take him out in your boat," said Tom.

"Yes indeed," said Mr Hamon. "Bert loved to go out in the boat. We used to go fishing, and we used to go swimming and into the caves."

"Are there any caves you can drive into with your boat?" asked Tom.

"Not now I can't," said Mr Hamon sadly. "I'm too old now. But in those days, yes, there were three or four you could nose into, if the tide was right and not too much swell. Some of them go right back, you know, three or four hundred feet. I didn't like it in there, to be honest. Pitch black, and the thought of all that weight of rock over your head."

"Do you know if the caves were actually used for

smuggling?" asked Tom.

"Oh yes. Pirates and smugglers," said Mr Hamon. "But that was before my time. We never found anything much. But we did find our own secret cave though. One which nobody else knows about, not even the ones who do the boat trips. It's only me and Bert Mahy knows about it, and Kaz of course, eh Kaz?"

The Islanders looked at Kaz and she smiled and nodded her head.

"A secret cave!" said Tom. "I wouldn't mind seeing that."

Mr Hamon laughed. "You remind me of Bert, come to think of it," he said. "You're not related are you? Well, I'll tell you what, Kaz will show it to you, if you like. I can't do it myself. I can't manage it up and down the cliffs, but Kaz has her own boat down at Havre Gosselin. She will take you, won't you Kaz?"

"Yes, if you like, Grandpa. But I think it's time you had a little rest now."

"It'll have to be today or tomorrow. She's off back to Guernsey after that," said Mr Hamon. "Yes. It'll be just like old times. I like the idea of that."

Kaz took Mr Hamon off for his nap and the others said goodbye to him.

"Nice meeting you," he said. "Give my regards to Bert. Tell him to come over and see me. It's ages since he was last here."

Chapter 11

The Monument

The Islanders were making ready to leave as Kaz returned.

"Can we help with the dishes?" said Shani.

"Yes, alright then," said Kaz. "I'll wash, you dry. Now, about seeing the cave."

"It's alright," said Tom. "We'd love to see it but we don't want to be a nuisance."

"It's not that," said Kaz. "The thing is, my boat's only small and there's no way we could all fit into it. Not safely, anyway, and I only have three lifejackets."

"And we'll have Bart as well from tomorrow, hopefully," said Anna.

"I can only really fit three onboard," said Kaz. "But I don't mind showing you the cave, honestly. I think my grandpa kind of likes the idea. But I can only take two at a time."

"Ladies first," said Ian. "I don't suppose there's really time now. Why don't you three girls go tomorrow? Tom and I will go and meet Bart."

"That's true. Someone will have to meet Bart, and we don't even know what time he's arriving yet" said Anna. "But that means you boys might not get to see the cave."

"Is there a way down to it overland?" asked Tom.

"Yeah, sort of," said Kaz. "But you'd never find it."

"What about if you showed us the way up from the cave? Then we could show the boys later," said Anna.

"That might work," said Kaz. "Okay, so we'll go tomorrow shall we girls? It might be quite nice if the weather holds."

"Yeah, girls' outing. Alright then," said Anna. "You're on."

They arranged to meet at the Pilcher Monument, at the top of the path leading down to Havre Gosselin.

"If we meet at 11am we should get there around low water, so that'll be ideal," said Kaz. "Bring your bathers. If it's sunny we can go for a swim."

Kaz had things to do, so they said goodbye, made a final fuss of Ben and then started off towards the main road.

"Where to now?" said Ian.

"It must be getting near lunch time," said Tom. "Let's find somewhere with a nice view and have our sandwiches."

"I wouldn't mind having a look for that Pilcher Monument," said Anna.

"Good idea," said Shani. "We don't want to get lost on the way there tomorrow, or we'll be late for meeting Kaz."

"Okay, the Pilcher Monument it is," said Ian, looking at the map. "It's not too far from here. We can take a short cut through here, where it says Happy Valley."

"Yes, I'd like to see Happy Valley," said Shani.

They reached the turn off shown on the map, turned left off the main road, and were taken through open fields along a winding grass path with wooden ranch fencing to one side.

"That must be Happy Valley, down there," said Shani, pointing at a pretty house at the head of a long valley leading down to the sea.

Tom thought this might be a cue for a song, so he gave it his best:

"I'm so happy, happy,

Happy, happy, happy,

I'm so happy, I'm in Happy Valley!"

"Aw, Tom!" the others groaned.

They reached the top of a field and suddenly the path came to an end. There was a gateway through the hedge on their left leading to a strange looking building with stone walls, hardly any windows, and a thatched roof. They didn't know whether they should be walking through this property or not, as there were no signs, but on the other side of it they came to another path.

"Eeny, meeny, miney, mo. Let's go right," said Ian.

Luckily the path led them onto another main road and they turned left for the Pilcher Monument. Soon, they saw it before them. A tall obelisk, beautifully built in cut granite blocks, standing on the highest point of the headland.

There were one or two people sitting on wooden benches on the approach to the monument and a driver turning his horse and carriage around while his passengers had gone to admire the view.

The Islanders walked up to the monument and started to read the inscription on the base of it. This took some time as it was quite lengthy, including quotations from the Bible.

"Oh, that's awful," said Anna, eventually. "Five people, and all of them drowned … 'embarked in a sailing gig from the bay below this spot … 1868 and all were lost during a squall of wind … with heavy rain and thick darkness."

Anna was so moved by the inscription that she felt unable to read any more aloud, and neither did any of the others except for Ian when he reached the final part: " 'Also to urge upon others through the grace and mercy of God our saviour CAUTION and WARNING:- Thy way is in the sea and thy path in the great waters and thy footsteps are not known.' … Well there you are then," he said.

Everyone was silent. They reflected on the tragedy which had happened so long ago, but had been brought so vividly back to life by the inscription they had read, and the loss and the grief of those left behind.

On the other side of the monument, facing the sea, was a vacant bench, and they slowly walked over and sat down. It was a full five minutes before Tom's thoughts returned to normal.

"Lunch time, I think," he said.

With some lunch inside them, and the beautiful scenery to enjoy, they started to feel better again."

"What a place to keep your boat," said Anna, thinking of Kaz. "No wonder she's a little on the serious side."

"I don't know if I really want to go boating tomorrow," said Shani.

"You don't have to worry," said Tom. "Boating is much safer than it used to be, with lifejackets and all that."

"And you'll be staying close inshore, I should think," said Ian.

There was a fine view over Brecqhou from the bench and they noticed how beautifully landscaped and neat and tidy it was.

Shani had wandered over towards the path which led down to the tiny harbour. "Look over there," she said, pointing across the bay. "Do you think those are the Gouillot caves?"

Ian looked at the map. "Looks like it," he said, walking over for a better view. "Wow, they're quite something, by the look of it, but I think you need climbing gear to get down to them, and a guide, which we don't have."

Anna and Tom joined them.

"Where shall we go now?

"We could take this other track," said Ian, "Leading over to Port de la Joument, and then join up with the main road and make our way back."

"We really need to pop into a shop as well," said Tom, "For some more bread and stuff."

The rest of the afternoon passed easily. They got lost several times along the way and hardly met a soul. The views were wild and windswept, and they felt more like their old explorer selves. At one point they emerged through a gateway to find themselves on top of a hill. The sight before and all around them was quite magnificent. It was like being on top of the world. The green fields of Sark sloping down to the cliffs, with Brecqhou, Herm, Jethou, Guernsey, Alderney, all artfully arranged, as if by some great magician, on a vast table cloth of sparkling blue green sea.

"I reckon there's no more beautiful place on earth than

Sark on a summer's day," said Tom.

On the way towards the Avenue they passed the Court of Chief Pleas (the Sark Parliament), the Sark Fire Station and the Church. They rested a while on the low wall of the graveyard and it was just then that Anna's phone rang.

"It's a text from Bart," she announced. "They're leaving really early tomorrow morning. Should arrive here by about mid-day."

"That's fine," said Ian. "Tom and I will go and meet him if you're not back by then."

Shani went to look at some of the names on the gravestones. "Look what beautiful names the ladies had," she said, "Angel, Henriette, and look, there are lots of surnames all the same."

The others walked over to where Shani stood reading out the names. She had problems with quite a few as they were mostly French and some of the gravestones were so old it was difficult to see what was written on them.

"Guille, Hamon, De Carteret, those are some of the old families of Sark," said Ian. "They could even have come over with the first Seigneur."

"When would that have been?" asked Anna.

"An awful long time ago. Something like the 1500's. They came over from Jersey, I think," said Ian.

"But we won't hold that against them," said Tom, with a smile.

When they reached the Island Stores, they stocked up with food and eventually made their way back to Little Sark by a different route which connected up with Dixcart Lane, so as to avoid the busier road. Approaching the Coupée,

Anna remembered the incident with the birdwatchers and she started to feel uneasy at the prospect of bumping into them at dinner. She mentioned her fears to Ian who was equally keen to avoid them.

"How about asking my parents if we can eat at Base Camp this evening?" she suggested to the others.

"Great idea," said Tom. "We've loads of baked beans and some nice fresh bread and butter now."

The others waited at Base Camp while Anna tried to persuade Mr and Mrs Riley that they would really be better off without the Islanders at table that night.

"A romantic meal for two?" said Mr Riley, looking at Mrs Riley. "Yes, it does have some appeal, don't you think, dear? And I can see what you mean about those heavy tins of baked beans. It would be a shame for the boys to have to carry them back."

Eventually Anna reappeared. "It took some doing, but I managed to swing it," she said. "Oh, and look, Mrs B gave me this envelope. She said it was a message from her cousin Robert, you know, Bob the boatman."

"Hey, that's really funny," said Shani. "Now we know Phil the fisherman, and Bob the boatman."

"Well let's just call him Bob, shall we?" said Anna opening the envelope which had 'Islanders' scrawled across the front. She read the contents and frowned.

"What does it say?" asked the others.

"I can't believe it," said Anna. "He's telling us to keep away from the birdwatchers."

They crowded around and read the note together.

"But he told us to keep an eye on them before," said

Tom.

" 'Have checked out Birdwatchers. They are genuine. Please keep out of their way.' " Ian read out aloud.

"I reckon they've got to him," said Anna. "Somehow or other they've got to him."

"There's no way they're genuine birdwatchers," said Tom. "We haven't seen them birdwatching once. Boat watching, maybe."

"Well, if he says we should keep away, maybe we should," said Ian.

"No way. There's something fishy going on here. I'm going to carry on watching them, if I get the chance," said Anna. "But I'll be more careful next time."

That evening they dined sumptuously on sausage and beans on thickly buttered toast. It took some time and skill on Ian's part to have everything ready at the same time, but he did manage it, and everyone was suitably impressed.

"Good idea of yours, Anna, to eat outside," said Shani. "It's so much nicer in the open air."

"Phwoar! That was brilliant, Ian," said Tom, rubbing his tummy contentedly. "Yeah, this is more like a proper expedition now."

"It will be tomorrow when Bart gets here," said Ian. "That'll be all of the Islanders back together again."

Chapter 12

Bart Sets Sail from St Malo

Bart's father had been working hard to prepare the new yacht for its journey to Guernsey, via Sark of course, to drop Bart off. The rigging and sails were all sorted, the electrical equipment checked over, the engine fuelled and tested. She was the latest thing in modern cruising yachts, about 10 metres long overall, with a fair turn of speed. She was well equipped, with in-mast furling for the mainsail and two headsails on self-furling gear.

"That gennaker might come in handy if the wind carries on from the south-west," said Bart's father.

The paperwork too had been accepted at last by French Customs and, after a final polish, the yacht had been craned into the marina and carefully tied up alongside a pontoon with plenty of fenders to protect her gleaming white topsides.

Bart had helped his father to plot the course from St Malo, making best use of the wind and tides.

We'll have to leave early, Bart," said his father. "Five hours before high water at Dover. That'll be 5am French time, 4am Guernsey time."

Bart didn't mind leaving early. He was so looking forward to his first proper sea voyage and, of course, he was longing to meet up with his friends in Sark. He was already awake when his father knocked on the door at 4am. He quickly washed and dressed and packed the last of his things into his kit bag.

Anne Marie had made coffee. It was too early for breakfast so she gave them bread and croissants to take with them and some more coffee in a thermos flask.

They crept quietly down the stairs from the apartment, so as not to disturb the other residents, and made their way out into the cobbled street. It was still dark and there was hardly any traffic on the roads as Anne Marie drove them over to St Servan and down to the Bas Sablons marina where the yacht was waiting for them. Bart's father made one or two final checks and started the motor, then they kissed Anne Marie goodbye, slipped the mooring ropes and motored slowly out over the marina gate.

There was no wind to speak of but, as they continued quietly on their way out through the channel towards the Ile de Cezembre, gradually they felt the breeze picking up and the motion of the sea building as they moved away from the shelter of the land. By the time they had cleared the lighthouse marking the end of the channel they had unfurled the sails and were able to switch off the motor.

"Okay, Bart," said his father, handing over the wheel. "Steer 325 degrees. The first thing we want to pick up is that waypoint off the South West Minquiers buoy. I'm just going down to have a look at the chart."

With that he climbed down into the cabin, leaving his son to steer the boat. Bart felt a thrill of excitement as he gripped the wheel and peered intently into the darkness ahead. Now they had cleared the lights of the St Malo approaches there was nothing much to see, but here and there, as his eyes grew accustomed to it, he could just make out some tiny flashing lights in the distance.

 He checked the compass ... 320°. Whoops, he thought to himself and quickly corrected back to 325°. His father was down below for what seemed like ages. When he eventually came up the inky blackness of the night was just starting to turn grey and they were getting quite close to one of the flashing lights on their port side.

"That's Le Vieux Banc, North Cardinal," said his father. "Quick flashing white. Okay, we must be pretty much on track."

The breeze was still light and the boat was sailing gently along on a broad reach. Gradually, the day was dawning. The sky was turning greeny grey and then a pale powdery blue. Bart could see more and more clearly, but, apart from the boat, the waves and the sky, in fact there was nothing much more to see. The coast of France had dipped below the horizon and there was no land to be seen, just miles and miles of endless sea in all directions and the two of them, Bart and his father, on what now felt to Bart like a very tiny almost insignificant sailing boat, alone and vulnerable in the vastness of the sea.

He shivered. He wasn't at all sure that he liked this feeling. Come on, he said to himself, pull yourself together. It's not as if we're crossing oceans anyway. It's only a short hop across the bay.

Then the sun appeared above the horizon, blood red at first, then fiery with orange and yellow, lighting up the sky and turning the cold grey sea to bright blue. This is more like it, thought Bart, and he started to relax in the warmth of the sun.

Another hour passed by.

"7 o'clock French time," said his father. "I think it's time we had a spot of breakfast, don't you, Bart?"

They tucked into the French bread spread with good French butter and had their croissants with jam and a cup of deliciously strong French coffee. Bart felt so much better after his breakfast and wondered why he had felt odd earlier on.

"Where are we now, pa?" he asked his father.

"Hmm, nearly 8. We should be approaching the South West Minquiers buoy. Go and have a look on the starboard bow, will you, Bart? And give us a shout when you see it."

Bart went up forrard and, shielding his eyes against the sun which was still low in the sky, he looked out across the sparkling waters and scanned the horizon.

"I think I can just see some rocks," he shouted, "But I can't see the buoy yet." Then, ten minutes later, "Yes, I can see it. Must be about a mile away to starboard."

"Well then, we're not doing too badly," said his father, "But there ain't much wind. I think we'll break out the gennaker, Bart, and get a bit of a move on."

Bart gave a hand to furl up the jib and unfurl the gennaker, which was a big powerful sail, something like a cross between a genoa and a cruising spinnaker. Bart winched in the sheet until the sail filled taut and stopped flapping. They felt the extra speed immediately as the yacht heeled a little more then dug in to plough a steady furrow through the water.

"Look at that," said his father, checking the plotter. "Six knots over the ground. That's not bad in these light airs. Mind you, we have the tide with us at the moment. That's giving us an extra knot."

Bart went back to his look-out duties. "Here comes the North West Minquiers. Hey, dad, that must be Jersey over there."

"Let's hope so," said his father jokingly, "Or something has gone seriously wrong. Right, Bart, we'd better change course now. We're well clear of the Minquiers so I'm going to head due North. That should take us all the way. Can you just pop down and get the tidal atlas for me. Have a look around while you're down there, she's pretty smart down below. Better take your shoes off though."

Bart climbed down the companion way and found himself in a surprisingly spacious and luxurious cabin. There was a chart table and galley on the right, all fitted out with a proper cooker, fridge, microwave and sink, a separate toilet and shower on the left, and a roomy dining area. Up in the bow was a superb master bedroom, and there were two further small cabins in the stern under the cockpit. There were soft carpets, beautiful honey coloured woodwork and matching leather upholstery on the seating. The cabin had that special brand new smell and Bart tiptoed carefully around so as not to leave any evidence of his having been there. He picked up the tidal atlas and took it up to his father.

"Wow! It's amazing down there isn't it?" he said. "I should think the new owner will be really pleased."

"Quite something isn't she?" said his father. "Not my kind of boat though. I prefer something with a little more character. But she is really easy to sail, I must say."

By this time they were drawing closer to Jersey but keeping well offshore to avoid any rough water off La Corbiere point. The boat was sailing steadily on and Bart thought to himself that she couldn't have had a better start for her maiden voyage.

"I think we'd better change to Guernsey time," said his father, adjusting his watch. "It's ten o'clock French time so that's nine o'clock in Guernsey."

Bart followed suit.

"Hey, Bart. What's that dead ahead?"

Bart scanned the horizon. He could see something that looked perhaps like an island in the distance and then more land further away to the left.

"Is that Sark, pa? And is that Guernsey on the left?"

Now Bart really was getting excited. Soon he would be landing on Sark and joining up with the Islanders. He wondered how much of the island they had already explored. He was sure they would have lots to tell him. What a pity he hadn't been there at the start, but then he would have missed out on time spent with his father and on the sea trip which he was now really starting to enjoy.

They sailed along the west coast of Jersey with its long sweep of sand, the five mile beach.

"How about a coffee, Bart?" said his father. "I think there might be one left in the flask."

The time was coming up to 11am and they were about

level with Grosnez point when the wind started to ease. The sails were not holding their shape as they had done, every now and then they flapped a little and the boat felt noticeably slower.

"That's just what we don't need," said his father, checking their slower progress on the chart plotter. "Tide's changing now. We're going to be punching it from now on and the wind seems to be giving up on us."

They tried poling out the gennaker, and motor sailing, but in the end the wind dropped completely and they had to furl the sails and use the engine for the last part of their journey.

Back at Base Camp 1, earlier that morning, Ian and Anna had woken first as usual but slightly later than the previous mornings. Anna didn't feel like painting. She planned to take her sketch pad with her on Kaz's boat later on. Ian wasn't keen on spying on the birdwatchers so they sat outside and chatted while the others came to.

"I've just realised," said Anna. "Bob didn't say we should keep away from the black boat. I wonder if that means something."

"But the black boat has gone anyway," said Ian. "We saw it going over towards Guernsey and we haven't seen it since."

"That's true," said Anna. "We'll have to keep an eye out for it though, when we go out with Kaz. I'm really looking forward to that now. Looks like a nice day for it."

"Should be good for Bart too," said Ian. "I wonder if

they've left St Malo yet."

Eventually the others appeared and so did Mrs B with the breakfast box.

"Morning, campers," she said. "Lovely weather isn't it? Any plans for today? Oh yes, doesn't your friend arrive today? Has he brought a tent, do you know? If he hasn't, I'm sure we can rustle up another tent from somewhere."

"I think he has his own," said Anna. "That was the plan, anyway."

"Oh jolly good. Well, I shall look forward to meeting him later," said Mrs B as she shot off back along the path.

At the hotel, Mr Riley was feeling very mellow. He had slept soundly and was now recovering after a full cooked breakfast with Sark eggs, bacon, tomato and sausage, and, as a special treat, Mrs Riley had allowed him a slice of fried bread. "But we will be walking it off later," she promised, as she returned to their room to dress for the day.

Mr Riley asked for another cup of coffee. "I think I'll take it outside if you don't mind," he said to the waiter. He sauntered out into the garden and found himself a sunny spot at one of the tables. His coffee arrived. He stretched, sat back and relaxed and was just thinking that surely life could not be any better than this, except perhaps it would be nice to have a newspaper to read, when Anna and Shani appeared.

Anna had been thinking about the boat trip and whether she should mention it to her parents. She was in two minds about it. On the one hand, her parents might not allow her to go, and on the other, there would be hell to pay if they found out she had gone without asking. In the end she knew what she had to do and she asked Shani to come with her for moral support. Seeing her father sitting at the table she thought how relaxed and how well he looked.

"Father," she said, kissing him on the cheek, "You're looking really well this morning. You look ten years younger."

Mr Riley beamed at his daughter. "Flattery will get you everywhere," he said, but he knew his daughter well and he sensed there was a purpose to this visit. "And I must say you two girls are looking mighty fine too. So tell me, what is it I can do for you this fine morning?"

Anna told him about the boat trip, being careful to mention how experienced Kaz was, that they would stay close inshore and there were lifejackets onboard.

Mr Riley looked serious.

"Oh, I don't know if your mother would allow that," he said.

Luckily, Mrs B was standing nearby, instructing one of the gardeners, and she had overheard some of their conversation.

"Kaz Hamon, is that?" she said. "Going out with Kaz are you? Well you won't find anyone better. Yes, goodness me, she's been going out in boats since she was a baby."

Mr Riley wavered.

"Do you really think they would be absolutely safe?" he asked Mrs B.

"The Hamons have lived here for nearly 500 years," she said. "I think they know their way around by now."

Mr Riley nodded thoughtfully.

"Well, that's alright then," he said, "But do be careful now or you'll have your mother down on us like a ton of bricks."

His daughter embraced him. "Thank you, father," she said delightedly.

"Thank you, Mr Riley," said Shani, and they ran off to tell the others.

I do hope I've done the right thing, Mr Riley thought to himself.

By the time the Islanders were ready to leave Base Camp it was half past nine.

"It'll never take us an hour and a half to walk to the monument," said Shani.

"No, but I want to leave now, before mother gets wind of it," said Anna.

"We only have to go to Port Gorey to meet Bart," said Ian, "And there's no point in getting there too early. We might as well come with you for the outing."

"Thank goodness Bart is finally on the way," said Tom. "We really can't leave our exploring any longer."

They took the usual packed lunches and the girls took their swimming things. They had just reached the Coupée when Anna's phone went off. "Blast! I know who that is," she said.

Chapter 13

Three Girls in a Boat

"Now, Anna, that was very naughty of you, taking advantage of your father like that."

"Sorry, mother."

"If it had been up to me I most certainly would not have given permission, but as your father has allowed it, well, so be it."

"Yes, mother."

"But you really must promise me you will be careful, and if you are in any danger at all you must phone me straight away."

"Yes, mother, I promise ... Yes, I will be careful ... Sorry, mother ... Yes, I will ... Okay then ... Okay then ... Bye bye ... Yes, sorry ... bye bye."

She switched off. "Phew, that was pretty close," she said to the others.

They stopped at the Coupée, as there was plenty of time to enjoy the view.

"No sign of the birdwatchers," said Ian.

"Nor the black boat," said Tom. "Cor, I really thought

we might be onto something there. I thought it might be the start of something but it's all gone quiet."

"Never mind," said Shani. "Now that Bart is arriving maybe we can get on with some serious exploring. There's lots of the island we haven't seen yet."

Ian and Tom walked with the girls until they reached the turn off to Happy Valley.

"Hope you have a great time with Kaz," said Ian.

"Yeah, I'm really jealous," said Tom. "I'm longing to hear all about the cave. Try and find a way down to it, if you can, then we can all go down together. I'm sure Bart would like to see it too."

Anna and Shani strolled off in the direction of the monument. There was no hurry, they still had plenty of time. They took the same path as the previous day, through the fields and past the funny little thatched house, and they chatted happily together as they went. Then, as they approached the monument, they saw Kaz, and Ben the dog, waiting for them, so they hurried up towards them. Kaz had a bag over her shoulder and was carrying a small petrol can. Ben, who was on his lead, started to jump up and down with excitement as soon as he saw them, whining and wagging his tail.

"Hello, Kaz," said Anna, making a fuss of the dog. "Is Ben coming too? There's a good boy, Ben! You did say eleven, didn't you?"

"Yeah, but I managed to get away early," said Kaz, "So I thought I might as well come here and wait for you. Here, can you take Ben. Be careful though, he's pulling like mad this morning."

Shani took hold of Ben, who lolloped about wagging his tail, panting and grinning.

"I think he knows where we're going, don't you, Ben?" said Kaz.

They walked past the monument and down to the top of the path. Anna and Shani could not help thinking of the boating party which had walked this very way, all those years ago, and what had befallen them. Anna shivered slightly and looked over towards Guernsey. There was some low cloud in that direction but over Sark the sun was shining and the sky was blue. There had been a breeze earlier but it had died away and the sea was calm.

"It's a perfect day for it," said Kaz.

They started down the steps along a zig zag path leading to the little harbour.

"I forgot to ask," said Anna. "Do you have sails on your boat?"

"No. Outboard motor and oars," said Kaz. "Look. You can just see her now, down there."

She stopped and pointed to a sturdy looking small fishing boat, painted bright red outside and pale blue inside.

"Isn't she lovely," said Shani.

"Yep. She's my pride and joy," said Kaz.

They climbed down the final run of steps onto a tiny quay. Kaz untied a rope and pulled her boat in to the steps leading down into the water. "Come on then, Ben. In you go," she said. "Okay, Anna, if you'd like to get in as well and hang on to Ben. That's it. And if you can just hold onto the boat, Shani, I'll start her up." She put the petrol can under the rear seat. "I always bring some spare fuel," she said. "Just in case." She unhooked the motor, lowering the propeller into the water, fiddled with the choke and throttle and pulled on the starter cord. The motor immediately burst into life and Kaz beamed proudly at the others. It was the first time they had really seen her smile.

"She always starts first or second pull," said Kaz. "Okay, girls. If you want to hop in. The lifejackets are in that locker up front."

They donned their lifejackets.

"There's no lifejacket for Ben," said Shani.

"Don't worry about him," said Kaz. "He can swim like a fish."

Ben stood on the front seat, with his front paws on the foredeck. He stared attentively over the bow and sniffed the sea air.

Kaz pushed them away from the quay with the boathook and, taking control of the motor, steered them out of the little harbour. "Right," she said, looking at her watch, "We're nice and early. Fancy a trip around Brecqhou first? Then we'll make our way over to the cave."

For a moment, Anna wondered whether this might be against the rules.

"Don't worry," said Kaz, noticing Anna's expression, "We can stay close in all the way round. You'll be safe as houses."

The little red boat was called *Lazy Daisy*. She burbled happily out of the bay and into the Gouillot passage, between Sark and Brecqhou, where the cliffs towered above them on both sides. Kaz had to turn the throttle to full speed to fight against the tide. It felt as if they were racing through the water but their progress, measured against the rocks on either side, was fairly slow. It reminded Anna of the time she had gone swimming with Shani off Shell Beach in Herm, and got into trouble*.

They reached the end of the passage and turned to port, taking them out of the tidal race and along the north side of Brecqhou. They came level with the castle and as they were even closer to it than when they had passed by in *Cobo Alice*, they were able to see it in more detail. They were chatting about the castle and the winding roadway leading up to it, how they were all built of granite and how much it must have cost when, in the distance, they heard a dull, throbbing sound, like the beating of wings against the sky, fading from time to time, then getting louder. They turned to face the sound. Anna and Shani were amazed to see a helicopter approaching fast from the north and heading straight for them.

"Quick, grab hold of Ben!" said Kaz.

Shani lunged out and caught hold of his collar, pulling him back into the boat. The noise grew louder and louder into a roaring crescendo as the helicopter hovered directly above them. They crouched down instinctively as if flattened by the rush of wind from its beating rotor blades. Then it passed over, continued on its way and disappeared from sight.

Gradually the noise of the helicopter subsided and peace was restored. Ben had been trembling with fear in the bottom of the boat, and Shani, who was starting to get rather fond of him, gave him a hug to let him know he was safe now.

They continued quietly on their way around the western tip of the little island. Anna and Shani were amazed at how Kaz steered *Lazy Daisy* through the rocks, threading her way amongst them and, in some cases, missing them only by inches but still with deep water under her keel.

Turning the corner and heading back towards Sark, they came across a tiny harbour with a pier and a small crane.

"This is where they land their supplies," said Kaz.

Heading back towards the Gouillot Passage, they passed an enormous cave.

"Is your cave as big as that?" Shani asked Kaz.

Kaz wrinkled her nose. "Naahh," she said dismissively, "But it's much better than that one. You'll see."

The *Lazy Daisy* was heading back into Havre Gosselin. Anna and Shani thought for a moment that Kaz was abandoning the trip and taking them back, but at the last minute she veered to starboard. They shot through a narrow passage between two rocks and then continued along the coast, close inshore, heading south towards Little Sark.

After leaving the girls, Ian and Tom had gone back to Base Camp 1. Ian had wanted to collect the leaflet on the Silver Mines. "If we get there early, we can have a look at the mines in waiting for Bart to arrive," he said.

They took the path for Port Gorey and soon reached

the cliff top above the bay. It was at the spot where they had first seen the black boat at anchor, but, looking down, the bay was empty and there were no boats to be seen. Tom scanned the horizon, looking over towards Jersey. "Wait a minute, Ian," he said. "I think I can see something heading this way."

Ian fetched out the telescope and handed it to Tom.

"Yes," said Tom, adjusting the focus. "It's a yacht, I think, but it isn't sailing. It's motoring this way."

"How far away do you think they are?" asked Ian.

"Hmm, I reckon it's about 15 miles to Jersey from here, but the tide's against them now," said Ian. "If it is them, I should think it will take them two or three hours to get here."

"Cor, you're good at your maths," said Tom. "It's a mystery to me how you do it, Ian. Still, that gives us plenty of time to look at the Silver Mines on the way down, then we can sit and have our lunch over by the landing place."

Ian laughed. "It's not even eleven o'clock yet and you're already thinking about lunch, Tom," he said.

"Too true!" said Tom. "Eleven is it? Must be time for elevenses I think."

The girls, by now, were well on their way to the secret cave, but only Kaz knew where it was and she was keeping it to herself. They had motored close inshore past the Victor Hugo cave, Port és Saies and Grande Grève, and Kaz had told them stories about each place on the way. Ben the dog was starting to enjoy himself. He sat between his two new friends gazing up adoringly at them in turns and giving them affectionate licks.

"Doesn't he have such beautiful brown eyes?" said Anna.

Kaz looked reprovingly at him. "He's a mad dog, aren't you Ben?" she said, and Ben wagged his tail and scrambled over to her, just to show he still loved her too.

They approached a rocky headland and, as they rounded it, a small sandy beach came into view.

"Blast! What's he doing there?" said Kaz. She cut the engine and *Lazy Daisy* slowed right down. Ahead of them, some thirty or forty metres away, was a larger vessel, lying stationary in the middle of the bay. She had a blue hull and white topsides, a fore-cabin with a small wheelhouse and a large open cockpit.

Anna and Shani looked at Kaz.

"It's Bob Baker doing one of his boat trips," she said. "He doesn't normally stop here like that though."

"Do you mean Bob the boatman? The one who is also the Constable?" said Shani.

"Yeah. Do you know him then?" said Kaz, looking ahead at the boat as if wondering what to do. "We'll just hang about here for a while. He'll probably move on in a minute. Just chuck the anchor over will you, Anna, and we'll pretend we're fishing. Hang on to Ben, Shani!"

Ben had become excited at the sight of Anna swinging the anchor and was making ready to dive in after it. Shani managed to stop him just in time and settled him back down in the boat.

Kaz prepared her fishing rod and Anna peered over at

the blue boat to see if it was the same Bob that they had met earlier, or cousin Robert as Mrs B called him. Surely there couldn't be too many boatmen in Sark called Bob, she thought to herself. She could make out three figures in the boat: one man in the stern and yes, she did recognise him, and two men standing up, looking intently at the beach. One of them had a camera, or something, and the other was looking through binoculars. "Good grief!" she said suddenly. "It's the birdwatchers, Shani." She plonked herself down and pulled her sunhat down over her eyes.

"What's up?" said Kaz.

"It's the birdwatchers," said Shani. "We've been spying on them and Anna got into trouble."

"Oh right," said Kaz. "So you don't want them to know it's you?"

"No... yes ... that's right," hissed Anna from the bottom of the boat.

"Look out then, they're on the move," said Kaz, watching the blue boat which had started to move out of the bay and was heading straight for them. Then they heard a voice.

"Whaddo, Kaz ... Out fishing, is it? Caught anything yet?" Bob called out cheerily.

"No, nothing yet, Bob," Kaz called back.

The blue boat came level with them and Shani looked away so she might not be recognised either. Anna lay in the bottom of the boat pretending to sunbathe.

"Girls' outing is it?" Bob shouted above the noise of the motor. "Have a nice one. Good luck with the fishing."

Then the boat had passed them by and they were

left bobbing in its wake as it motored out towards the headland. The birdwatchers were deep in discussion and hardly seemed to notice *Lazy Daisy* and her crew.

Kaz waited a minute for them to disappear from sight.

"Well, what was all that about?" she said.

Anna and Shani explained how Bob had asked them to keep an eye on the black boat and the birdwatchers, but then had left them a note telling them to keep away, and how Anna and Ian had been caught out and shouted at.

"You've certainly been pretty busy," said Kaz.

"Do you think we can trust Bob?" said Anna. "We were sure something was going on between the birdwatchers and the men on the black boat. You don't think they might have got to him do you?"

"What, you mean paid him off? Bribed him or

something like that? No, not Bob," said Kaz. "He's a sound enough bloke. There's no way he would do anything like that. Maybe they are just birdwatchers."

"If you'd been watching them like we have, you wouldn't think that," said Shani.

Kaz thought about it for a moment. "Beats me," she said. "Anyway, we'd better be getting on if we want to catch the tide." She started the engine and gave the order to haul up the anchor, then drove them towards the beach. Just before they reached the shore she switched off the motor and tilted it, to keep the propeller clear of the sand. *Lazy Daisy* drifted gently in.

Chapter 14

The Secret Cave

Ben could hardly contain his excitement, now they were approaching dry land. "You can let him off the lead, Shani," said Kaz. He barked, jerked free, leapt over the bow of the boat and swam ashore, grinning at them.

"Okay girls, this is it," said Kaz, as *Lazy Daisy* bumped and turned broadside on to the beach. They had taken their shoes and socks off and were ready to lower themselves over the side of the boat and wade through the gently breaking surf up onto the beach. Kaz took the anchor with her and stuck it firmly in the sand higher up.

Anna and Shani looked around. It was a secluded little bay with steep cliffs on all sides. There was no sign of a cave. The water over the sand was an even brighter shade of turquoise than usual and crystal clear. Further up the beach were some strange tall rocks, almost like columns.

Kaz gave them one of her curious half-smiles. "Not bad, eh?" she said.

"It's so beautiful," said Shani quietly, "And so peaceful."

They stood silently for a moment but the peace was soon shattered by Ben barking excitedly from amongst the rocks further up the beach. He reappeared carrying a stick of seaweed.

"He wants you to throw it for him," said Kaz, "But you have to wrestle it off him first."

Anna tugged at the seaweed. Ben growled and pulled back. Anna growled too and tugged harder, shaking it from side to side. Ben hung on gamely but eventually let go. Anna turned and threw the stick as far as she could out into the water. Ben careered off, barking madly, dived into the sea, doggy paddled his way out to grab the stick and returned triumphantly to drop it at Anna's feet.

This game was repeated several times, with Anna and Shani taking it in turns, until Kaz advised them to ignore him or they would have to carry on all day. "Come on," she said, "It's time I showed you the cave."

They followed her up the beach, leaving Ben to wrestle with his stick. She led them amongst the tall rocks up to the very top of the beach where the sand was soft and dry. "There you are," she said. "See anything?"

They looked around. Over to one side was a gully, heaped up with rocks and boulders which had fallen in. On the other sides the cliff face had been hollowed out here and there, but there was nothing that looked like a cave.

Kaz laughed.

Anna and Shani were beginning to think it might be some kind of joke.

"Come on then," said Kaz. "I'll put you out of your

misery. Follow me."

She took a torch out of her pocket and walked towards one of the hollows at the base of the cliff. It was not until they were actually standing in the hollow that they could see, tucked away in the left hand corner, a jagged hole, about the size of a doorway, leading into darkness.

Kaz shone the torch to show the way. Once they were inside, the cave opened up into a bigger tunnel with a soft sandy floor and after they had felt their way carefully along this, for some ten to fifteen metres, the tunnel widened out into an inner chamber about the size of a large room.

Anna and Shani had not said a word. Kaz plonked herself down on the sandy floor. "So. What do you think of it?" she said, shining the torch on the walls and roof of the cave.

"It's amazing," said Anna, in a whisper.

Shani wasn't sure what to say. She thought back to what Kaz's grandfather had said about not feeling too comfortable in the caves. She too could feel the weight of the rocks. It felt as if they were pressing in on her. She started to feel hot and prickly and short of breath. She tried to fight it off but she couldn't help it. She was gripped by a horrible sickly fear. "I'm sorry. I can't stay in here," she blurted out. She staggered to the wall of the cave and started to feel her way out.

"It's okay," said Kaz, quickly scrambling to her feet and shining the torch towards the mouth of the cave.

Anna took hold of Shani's arm, to help her, and, as quickly as they could, they made their way out.

Reaching daylight and gasping in the fresh air, Shani

had never felt so relieved in her life. "Oh ... Oh ..." with each breath, was all she could say. She held onto Anna and after a minute or two she started to regain her composure. "Oh ... I'm so sorry ... I don't know what came over me."

"Don't worry about it," said Kaz, patting her on the shoulder. "Lots of people are affected like that."

Ben, who had been exploring on the rocks, came over to see what all the fuss was about. He cocked his head over to one side, whined, wagged his tail and waggled up to Shani to comfort her.

"It was really amazing though," said Anna. "Thanks for showing us, Kaz."

"You haven't seen it all yet," said Kaz. "There's another tunnel which goes off to one side and comes out further down the beach."

"Wow. I'd love to see that," said Anna. "How come we missed that. I didn't notice anything to one side."

"Count me out," said Shani, who was just starting to turn a better colour. "You go, Anna. I'll just stay here for a while. Ben will keep me company, won't you Ben?"

Ben wagged his tail, then shivered and gave himself a huge shake, showering them all in wet sand, which they found quite hilarious.

Anna and Kaz returned to the cave and, sure enough, in the darkest part of the tunnel Kaz revealed a narrow fissure just wide enough for a person to slide through, and beyond this another tunnel, but this time with a rocky floor strewn with pebbles sloping down to the far end some fifteen to twenty metres away, where daylight shone in.

Anna followed Kaz to the end where they clambered out onto some rocks and into the sunshine. Then they were able to climb over the rocks, around the side of a rock pool and back onto the sandy part of the beach, where they were spotted by Shani and Ben who came down to join them.

"It's fantastic, Shani," said Anna. "Come on, you really must have a look."

"No thanks," said Shani. "I'll take your word for it. But I'll tell you what: I don't think the cave is as much of a secret as you think, Kaz. Look what I've found." She held up an empty cigarette packet.

"Oh? Let's have a look," said Kaz. "Where did you find this?"

"Just by the entrance to the cave," said Shani. "I was sitting on that stone, where you left me, and I looked down and there it was, in this gap between some rocks."

"French cigarettes," said Anna, inspecting the packet. "No sign of water damage, so it wasn't washed up by the sea. Looks quite recent. It doesn't mean to say they found the cave though."

"Well, I suppose other people are bound to have found it by now," said Kaz. "But they'd have to come in by boat though. I can't really see anyone finding a way down from the top. It was probably some French yachtsman who dropped that."

"Or the men on the black boat," said Shani. "They were French, remember? Well, flying the French flag anyway."

"That's true," said Anna, handing the cigarette packet

back to Shani. "Better keep that as evidence, Shani, just in case. I still think they were up to something, them and the birdwatchers. Let's have a good look around and see if we can find anything else."

"You know what?" said Kaz. "The cave would be perfect for smugglers or anything like that. I'll go and check it out. If someone has been in there, we should be able to see."

"The trouble is," said Anna, "We've all gone tramping in and out ourselves, so it'll be our footprints all over the place."

Anna and Shani searched the beach while Kaz went back into the cave. She searched every corner with her torch. The sandy floor was too dry to show any footprints. It looked as if it had been disturbed, but that was probably by her and the others. She wondered whether things remained exactly as they were left each time the cave was visited. If so, some of the marks in the sand might have been made by her father, or her grandfather. It was an interesting thought but there were no signs, really, of foul play, so she gave up and went to find the others.

Ben had been helping Anna and Shani to search the beach. He had found several interesting lengths of seaweed which he took over to show the others but, apart from that, they found nothing else and all of them were starting to feel hungry.

"If we're going for a swim, we'd better go first before we eat," said Kaz.

It was just after mid-day and the sun was at its hottest, warming the water as it crept up slowly over the hot sand. *Lazy Daisy* was afloat, so they pulled her back into the beach with the anchor rope, took their swimming things and changed out of their clothes. Ben found a shady spot and settled down for a nap.

They had a lovely peaceful swim, lying in the warm shallow waters mostly, and chatting. Anna thought how quiet it was without the boys to shout and splash about. "I wonder if Bart has arrived yet?" she said.

They explained to Kaz about Bart and how he was due to arrive from St Malo.

"I'd like to come exploring with you," said Kaz, "But I have to get back to Guernsey tomorrow. Mind you, I know where everything is on Sark anyway, so there wouldn't be much point really."

"Yes, but you'd make a fantastic guide," said Shani. "I mean, just look at this place. We'd never have found it without you. And Ben could come too. Wouldn't that be nice?"

They had their lunch, sharing some tasty titbits with Ben, and then Anna asked Kaz if they could try to find a way up from the beach.

"There's only one way up really," said Kaz. "It's quite tricky but I'll show you if you like."

There was a large rock on one side of the beach which, over time, had become separated from the cliff alongside. The gully between it and the cliff was partially filled with boulders and stones which had been washed into it or fallen from the cliffs above. The seaward side of this rock sloped down, so that they were able to climb up and over the top of it, and then down over the boulders which bridged the chasm, and then up and to the right, along a narrow ledge which led them up to the headland at the top. Then they had to pick their way through a thick patch of gorse and brambles until they reached a barbed wire fence with a field beyond.

It was not too difficult a climb but you would never know it was possible if you were looking down from the cliff top.

"The trouble is, we'll never find it," said Anna, looking around for some distinguishing feature of the place.

"We'll have to leave a marker," said Shani.

They searched their pockets for something suitable and Kaz found a piece of string which they tied to the barbed wire fence.

"We'll have to remember it's about 6 metres, well, four fence posts in from the corner of the field," said Anna. "How do you get back to the road?" she asked Kaz.

"Just follow the hedge along there and then you'll come to a stile," said Kaz. "At least, there used to be a stile, then it's over that and you'll see a gateway on the far side of the field."

They admired the view from the cliff top, then made their way carefully back down to the beach. Ben led the way, running ahead, then scrambling back to see why it was taking them so long.

Tom and Ian had gone first to see the chimney of the silver mine which was perched high up on the cliffs. It was sturdily built of granite, with tapered sides, in the shape of an upturned bucket.

"I suppose this must have been for ventilation," said

Ian. "There must have been a shaft going all the way from here down into the mine and then, when you think, Tom, they dug out all of the shafts of the mine right down to below sea level. It must have been incredibly hard work."

"Let's have a read of the leaflet," said Tom.

They sat down by the chimney. Ian kept an eye on the distant, approaching yacht while Tom read from the leaflet.

"They started in 1833, and there were at least 75 miners," said Tom. "Cor, just imagine that. It says here there were 172 people living on Little Sark. It must have been really quite busy … and there was a narrow gauge railway, and a jetty to load up the ships."

They looked down at the bay, trying to visualise how it had been.

"It's incredible isn't it?" said Ian, "Because there's hardly anything left of it now. That old ruin down there must have been the pump house, I reckon."

They looked through the telescope at the yacht which was slowly inching its way towards Sark.

"It has to be Bart," said Tom. "There's no sign of any other boats coming this way."

Tom finished reading the leaflet. "Cor, some of it was 120 metres below sea level, Ian. It's really sad how it all ended though … and it says here … IMPORTANT. It is dangerous to explore it. We have to keep strictly to the paths at all times."

"Well, it would be really stupid to try and go down into the mines," said Ian. "They say all of the shafts have been filled up anyway, but we can go down and see what's left of the old buildings."

They found a grassy path leading down towards the bay and came first upon the remains of the engine house. There was only one corner left standing which towered up above them, the rest was reduced to low walls and overgrown, but they could still make out the shape of it.

The path led them down along one sloping side of the inlet of the bay. Built into the slope and dotted along the path were the remains of other smaller structures.

"I expect these would have been for storage and workshops and things like that," said Ian. "And along this path was probably the route of the railway."

They reached the end of the path and picked their way over a flat expanse of rock, finally reaching the landing place, right at the end. This was not much more than a rusty old ladder and some other old bits and pieces of metal hammered into the rocks for tying up to.

All the while they had been keeping an eye on the white yacht which was now easily visible and only a few miles out.

"Let's try waving, Ian," said Tom.

So they jumped about and shouted and waved at the yacht.

"I hope it is him," said Ian, "Or we're going to look pretty silly."

They watched for a minute to see if they had been spotted but there was no sign of a response from the yacht, so they settled down to eat their lunch.

Chapter 15

Exploring Grande Grève

Onboard the yacht, Bart had mixed emotions. He had enjoyed the trip immensely, especially being together with his father, just the two of them, and he was also looking forward to Sark and meeting up with the rest of the gang, but amongst these pleasurable thoughts he also knew that soon he would have to say goodbye to his father, and he might not see him again for a long time. Even meeting up with the Islanders, he realised, would only be for a couple of days and then the girls would have to leave for England. Still, after Sark he would be staying with his grandmother in Guernsey, and perhaps he could spend some time with Ian and Tom.

His father noticed how Bart had gone quiet and gave him a hug. "Never mind, old chap," he said. "I'll be over at Christmas time for sure, and maybe we can get you over to St Malo before that, for a few days."

Bart swallowed hard and nodded.

"Tell you what," said his father. "If all goes to plan, we might do some proper cruising next year. There's a nice little ketch in Jersey I'm interested in. Needs a little tidying up, but if I can buy her at the right price, at the end of the season, I might snap her up. Then we can work on her over the winter and maybe cruise around the Islands next year, for a week or so."

"Wow. That would be really great, dad," said Bart, cheering up noticeably. "Could I bring some of my friends along?"

"Don't see why not," said his father. "It would be nice to have a proper crew for a change."

Bart smiled. He knew his father was teasing him. "Can I have a look through the binoculars, dad?" he said.

All the time, Sark was getting closer. Now, Bart could make out the individual rocks on the approach into Port Gorey, then he spotted something moving, closer in. "It's them!" he shouted. "They're waving."

"Get up by the mast and give them a wave back," said his father. "Be careful though. One hand for the boat and —"

"Yes, I know," said Bart, clambering up over the cabin top, "And one hand for yourself." He braced himself against the mast, stood up as straight as he could and waved with both arms outstretched.

Bart's father shielded his eyes and peered over towards the landing place. "Yep, they've seen you," he said, and laughed. "They're waving back like mad."

"It is them! It is them!" shouted Tom, jumping about in high excitement and waving frantically.

"Alright, Tom," said Ian looking through his telescope. "Yes, I can see Bart up by the mast. Wow, it's a lovely looking boat. She looks brand new."

The yacht completed the last few hundred metres of her maiden voyage, slipping in gently past Boue Tirlipois, just showing to port, and Grande Bretagne rock to starboard. Bart was up front, ready with the anchor. Some thirty or forty metres out his father gave the order to let go. There was a splash and the roar of chain over the bow roller, Bart's father reversed the boat to bed in the anchor, then switched off the engine.

"Ahoy there, Bart! Ahoy there, Mr Henry!" shouted Tom and Ian from the landing place.

"Be with you in a minute, lads," shouted Mr Henry.

Bart helped his father to launch the rubber dinghy and, after a quick once over to make sure everything was ship-shape, they stepped in and Bart rowed them ashore. They climbed up the ladder to a rousing welcome.

"Bart, we thought you'd never get here! Hello Mr Henry. Nice boat, does she go well? Did you have a good trip?"

"Good to see you, lads," said Mr Henry, shaking hands with Ian and Tom. "Yes, lovely trip thank you. Could have done with a little more wind though."

"Are you coming ashore?" said Tom.

"No, I'm sorry, lads. I wish I could, but the new owner will be waiting for me in Guernsey. I'm supposed to get there by two, so I'd better crack on."

"Cheerio, pa," said Bart, giving his father a last hug.

"Goodbye, son. Have a great time on Sark. See you soon."

It was quiet for as moment. Neither of them said

anything.

"Go on, off you go. Oh look now, I nearly forgot." His father handed over an envelope. "Here's some pocket money. Now have a great time. Don't spend it all at once." He climbed down the ladder, shoved off and rowed back to the yacht.

"Come on, Bart," said Tom, trying to cheer him up. "We've got lots to show you. Did you know this was the landing place for the silver mine?"

They walked back over the rocks to the path. Bart turned for a last wave to his father, who had started the engine and was just stowing the anchor. He gave a last, big wave back and then hurried back to the helm, to steer the boat out of the bay.

"Silver mine eh?" said Bart.

"Yes," said Ian. "Look, we bought this leaflet about it from the tourist office."

Bart looked at the leaflet. "Sark is a pretty interesting place, isn't it? To say it's so small, there's an awful lot that's happened here."

"Yeah, we've got lots to tell you as well," said Tom.

"Where are the girls?" asked Bart.

Ian and Tom told Bart about Kaz and the secret cave.

"So they're out in Kaz's boat? Lucky things," said Bart.

"Well, you've just had a trip over from St Malo," said Tom. "How lucky was that?"

"Yeah, well actually it was pretty exciting," said Bart, "But it was so boring with all of those delays, and waiting for the paperwork."

"Yes, you said. That's when you were reading the French newspapers," said Ian.

"Oh, that's right, I told you," said Bart. "It's a good way to learn French though and there was one interesting article. Did I tell you about the burglars who vanished into thin air?"

"I don't think so," said Tom.

"Well, I was talking to Anne Marie about it, and she helped me to translate it, to be honest. Anyway, she said there were only two roads leading to this property and the police had road blocks on both of them."

"But the thieves still managed to escape?" said Ian.

"Yes, but it's pretty obvious how they did it really," said Bart. "They must have had a boat."

"What sort of boat?" said Tom.

"I don't know what sort of boat," said Bart, "But the property is right overlooking the beach, so it would make sense, wouldn't it, to use a boat."

"I wonder if the police have thought of that," said Ian. "Maybe you should have told them, Bart."

"No, Anne Marie reckons they probably knew how it was done but they're keeping it quiet."

Ian and Tom were pleased to see that all of this talk of mysterious happenings in the night had taken Bart's mind off things, and he had now cheered up considerably. They showed Bart around the ruins of the silver mine and then started along the steep path up the hill in the direction of the camp site.

"Any plans for today?" asked Bart.

"We thought we'd give you a hand to pitch your tent,

then maybe get on with some exploring," said Ian.

"We've been waiting for you to arrive before we really started on it," said Tom.

"How about going down to Grande Grève?" Ian suggested. "We haven't explored that yet and the tide should still be fairly low. That's where some people have found gemstones at low tide."

"Let's take our bathers and we can go for a swim," said Tom.

The sun was high in a cloudless sky, beating down on them, and it was hot and thirsty work climbing up from Port Gorey, especially for Bart with his camping gear, so Ian carried the tent and Tom took turns at carrying his kitbag. They reached the top and stopped to drink from their water bottles. Bart was amazed at the view. "Wow. You can see so much more from up here," he said. "Guernsey, Herm and Jethou, Jersey, even the coast of France way over there."

It was about one o'clock by the time they reached the campsite.

"We'd better get cracking or we'll miss the tide," said Ian.

They hastily pitched Bart's tent, which was a green, dome shaped contraption which sprung up almost all by itself, dumped his kitbag inside, grabbed their swimming things and marched off purposefully through the hotel grounds and along the road to the Coupée.

There was no time to show Bart the sights, but he was impressed with Base Camp 1, and the quaintness of the hotel and its beautiful gardens.

"I wonder how the girls are getting on," said Ian.

"What time will they be back?" asked Bart.

"We don't really know," said Tom. "It depends on Kaz, I suppose."

"I could phone them, I suppose," said Bart, then he thought better of it. "No, it doesn't seem right somehow. I think I'll leave my phone for emergencies."

There was plenty to talk about along the way. Bart told them all about the yacht and his journey over from France. Ian and Tom told Bart about the old lady at Cliff Cottage, about Bob the boatman and how they had been spying on the birdwatchers and the black boat.

"Cool," said Bart. "I'd like to join in with that. What's happening at the moment?"

"Well, the black boat left the other day," said Tom.

"And we haven't seen the birdwatchers recently," said Ian.

"So things have gone quiet? Just my luck," said Bart. "Never mind though, seeing as we're right down south, here on Little Sark, if we're going exploring, how about an expedition up north?"

"Yeah, we could find the north pole of Sark," said Tom enthusiastically. "That's a really good idea, Bart. It is good to have you back with us."

"That's where the Boutique Caves are, up north," said Ian. "I'd really like to have a look at them too."

Arriving at the Coupée, they looked down onto Grande Grève to assess the state of the tide.

"Good, there's plenty of the beach still showing," said Bart.

"Come on then," said Tom.

They hurried over to the far end of the Coupée, unhooked the chain and filed through the gateway, then carefully hooked the chain back up and half walked, half trotted down the zig zag steps hewn out of the sheer rock face.*

"Cor, there's millions of steps," said Tom. "I'm going to count them on the way back up."

They reached the bottom of the steps but, as there was a group of people sunbathing nearby, Tom and Ian only exchanged quiet little yahoos as they ran out onto the sand. "Yahoo! Yahoo!" Then they all burst out laughing as they sounded so silly.

"Cor, what a drag, Ian," said Tom. "That would have been perfect for a massively loud one.

Bart was laughing too. "You really are mad, you two," he said. "Come on, shall we have a swim first?"

They found some dry rocks to leave their clothes on, changed and ran down into the sea.

"Aaarghh!" shouted Bart, as they splashed through the shallows. "It's colder than I thought it would be."

"Naah, come on Bart. In you go, or we'll grab you and throw you in," shouted Tom.

"Oh yeah? Just you come and try it!"

There was a fair amount of noise and fooling around, then they all had a proper swim.

"See, it's not too bad once you get used to it," said Tom, treading water.

"Mmm. Just so long as you keep on the move," said Ian.

They swam back to the beach and scoured the shoreline for gemstones. There was nothing to be found but the sun on their backs gradually dried them and warmed them up.

"Shall we have a look at the caves?" said Bart. "There's a really good one in that rock over there."

He pointed to a huge rock standing alone near the top of the beach. They walked over to it.

"There you are, look at this," said Bart

Tom and Ian were amazed to see a tunnel, leading from front to back, right the way through. The tunnel had taken the form of an arch, leaning to one side and leading up to a point about 3 metres high. The floor of the tunnel was of firm sand about 3 metres wide so there was ample room for them to walk through. To Ian and Tom it felt almost like being in a church, or a miniature cathedral, all the more wonderful because it had been formed by nature and not by man. They counted their paces through it.

"28, 29, 30," said Ian, reaching the other end.

"Cor, it's about 30 metres long," said Tom.

"I've never seen anything like this in my life," said Ian. "I can't imagine the girls will have seen anything better."

They walked around the rock and then back through the tunnel again, so that they emerged facing the upper end of the beach and the cliff face. Between them and the cliff face was a stretch of sand strewn with massive boulders and, in amongst the boulders, rock pools fringed with sea weed. As they came closer the cliff face towered above them like some huge primeval monster, its skin cracked and striated, pale grey with marbled veins of blood red, and at its base a pebble bank and a number of small hollows and caves.

"Wow, this is amazing," said Ian, rushing towards the biggest, darkest cave. Then he stopped suddenly.

"There's something in there," he said.

It looked like white shining lights at the very back of the cave.

The three boys stopped and stared into the gloom, not knowing whether to turn tail and run for it.

Then Bart laughed. "It's only bits of polystyrene," he said.

Sure enough, as their eyes adjusted to the darkness, Ian and Tom could make out the pieces of white plastic foam which must have been washed up and blown into the back of the cave. Somehow they seemed to pick up the light and shine it back.

They explored the caves and then walked back onto the beach where Tom spotted some drift wood tangled up in a length of thick blue rope. They went over to examine it and found it was part of a motor boat. They could see where the steering wheel had been and, above it, was the instrument panel and controls for the engine.

Bart looked at one of the dials. "Look, that shows the number of hours the engine had run before she went down, 1700."

"I wonder how she got wrecked," said Tom, "And where she came from."

"Could have been a local boat," said Ian. "If it gets really rough there isn't much shelter. She might have broken free from her mooring and got smashed up on the rocks."

The others said nothing, but, like Ian, they also hoped that no one had been onboard when she went down.

They walked back to the rocks where they had left their clothes and started to get dressed. As they were doing so they heard the sound of an outboard motor and, looking up, they saw a small bright red boat rounding the rocks off Little Sark and heading in towards Grande Grève.

"I wonder if it's the girls," said Ian.

"Let's go down and see," said Tom, "If it is, we can give them a wave."

They ran down to the water's edge and the boat came closer in.

"It must be them," said Bart. "Look, they're waving."

The boys waved back.

"Do you think they'll land on the beach?" said Tom, but the little boat slowed down and came to a halt some 40 metres out.

Shani was holding onto Ben to stop him from leaping overboard. Anna cupped her hands around her mouth and called out.

"We can't stop. We just wanted to say: hello Bart!"

"Hello Bart!" echoed Kaz and Shani.

"Come and meet us by the monument, if you like," Anna shouted.

Kaz wheeled the boat around and headed out again.

The boys waved them off.

"Nice boat," said Bart. "Pity she doesn't have any sails, but she looks a good sturdy little fishing boat."

They went back to put on their shoes and collect their

swimming things, then headed for the steps leading up to the Coupée. On the way up Tom counted them, every one. After each hundred he held out a finger and, by the time he reached the top, he had three fingers and twenty seven steps.

"That's 327," he said proudly as he stepped out onto the Coupée. "So it must be about 327 feet high, do you reckon, Ian?"

"Could be," said Ian. "Some of those steps were pretty steep."

"And there's the paths between the flights of steps too," said Bart. "They were mostly sloping upwards."

After a breather they headed off at a gentle pace towards the Pilcher Monument, but, way before they reached it, they met up with Shani and Anna, who had started to make their way back. They were delighted to see Bart and made a great fuss of him.

"Where's Kaz?" asked Tom.

"She's leaving tomorrow, so she had a few last minute errands to do," said Shani.

"She was sorry she couldn't meet you properly though, Bart," said Anna.

"And she hopes we can all meet up again. And so does Ben," said Shani.

The Islanders, now complete, walked together back across the Coupée to the camp site, chatting happily about their adventures of the previous summer and the adventures, hopefully, which were to come.

"The secret cave was just amazing," said Anna. "You wait till you see it."

"Well we found a cave too," said Tom, "And it had a monster at the back of it, with white shining eyes."

"You're just being silly, Tom," said Shani.

"No, honestly," said Tom.

"Yeah, that's right," said Bart. "A monster called Polly Styrene!"

Chapter 16

Planning an Expedition

They arrived at the camp site, and, after Bart had sorted out his tent, they went over to the hotel to meet up with Anna's parents.

Mr and Mrs Riley were pleased to meet Bart again. "Such a charming young man," Mrs Riley said later to Mr Riley. "Such delightful manners."

Mr Riley was secretly very relieved that the girls had returned safely.

After so much fresh sea air and such an exciting trip out with Kaz, Anna and Shani were actually feeling quite tired. They excused themselves and went back to their tent for some quiet time. The boys chatted with Mr and Mrs Riley, then Ian and Tom showed Bart around the hotel gardens.

In the road, just outside the hotel, they came upon a horse and carriage. Mrs B was talking to the carriage driver.

"Yes, the two Belgian gentlemen, the ones staying at Cliff Cottage. They're off to Guernsey tomorrow on the

9 o'clock boat."

Tom and Ian pricked up their ears.

"So if you can collect them here, shall we say at about five past eight?"

"Right ho, Mrs B," said the driver. He made a clicking noise, shook the reins, and the horse dutifully set off down the lane. Mrs B turned and smiled at them. "So this must be ... young Mr Henry, if I'm not mistaken." She shook hands warmly with Bart. "Very pleased to meet you, I'm sure. We had noticed you'd arrived. Ah yes, we don't miss much around here, you know. Yes, we noticed the green tent. It's really looking rather jolly over at the camp site isn't it. Blue, brown, green, nice and colourful. Well, I'm so sorry-" She started off towards the hotel reception. "Must dash. Just had some more people arrive. Nice to meet you though."

Bart was left wondering what had hit him.

Tom and Ian smiled. "That was Mrs B," said Tom.

"But did you hear what she was talking about, to the carriage driver?" said Ian.

"Yes," said Tom. "The birdwatchers are going to Guernsey."

"Yes, and didn't the black boat go off to Guernsey?"

"Well, yes, in that direction I suppose," said Tom.

"I reckon they're still following it," said Ian, "For some reason."

Bart could not quite follow their conversation. "So it's the birdwatchers who need a carriage, to take them to the 9 o'clock boat?" he said.

The others nodded.

"Maybe one of us should follow them to Guernsey and find out, for sure, what they're up to," said Bart.

"Don't forget, Bob the boatman told us to keep away from them," said Tom.

"We don't have the money, anyway," said Ian. "It costs over £20 there and back. And what about our exploring? We've only a few days left, you know."

They walked down towards the Fontaine with Bart and pointed out Cliff Cottage from a distance. Then they made their way back to Base Camp 1 and told the girls what they had heard about the birdwatchers.

"We simply have to follow them," said Anna. "What about if we all club together and one of us goes."

"But that means someone would be missing out on our expedition to the North Pole," said Tom.

"What expedition?" asked Anna.

They explained their plans to conquer the north end of Big Sark and find the Boutique caves.

"And anyway," said Bart, "Your parents would never let one of us go off by ourselves on the boat, Anna."

Anna frowned and was silent for a moment, searching desperately in her mind for a solution. "There must be some way we can do it," she said.

"Wait a minute," said Shani. "What about Kaz? She's going back to Guernsey tomorrow. She might be leaving on the same boat."

"That's a brilliant idea, Shani," said Tom.

"And it wouldn't cost us anything," said Ian, "Provided she's willing to do it."

"If you think about it," said Tom, "Bob didn't say

anything to Kaz about not following the birdwatchers, did he?"

"She'll probably be home by now. I'll try phoning her," said Anna.

Kaz had been meaning to leave on a later boat but, after much pleading and persuading by Anna, she finally agreed to catch the 9 o'clock and to see what the birdwatchers did after landing in Guernsey. "I can only do it for an hour or so," she said. "My mum will be collecting me at half past twelve, so I can't stay later than that."

"That's wonderful, Kaz. Thank you so much," said Anna, nodding excitedly to the others and mouthing "She's going to do it!"

"And can you phone and tell us what happened? ... That's great, Kaz. Thanks ever so much. Speak to you tomorrow then."

Mr and Mrs Riley insisted that all of the Islanders should join them for dinner that evening in the restaurant.

The birdwatchers put in an appearance and Bart was able to see them for himself. He thought they definitely had a different look about them, their features and the way they dressed, but he wasn't sure if they were as bad as the others had described them. They had a serious look about them and kept themselves to themselves, but that might have been because they found it difficult to speak in English.

After dinner, Ian and Tom showed Bart the plan of the silver mine.

Back at the campsite, they settled down early. They

wanted to be up in time to make sure that the birdwatchers did actually leave. After that they had a busy day of exploring ahead of them.

They all slept well except for Bart who was not used to the hard ground and strange surroundings. When he did eventually fall asleep he was restless and dreaming vividly of all that had happened, the sea voyage with his father, landing on Sark, but then things became confused. Instead of Ian and Tom, it was the birdwatchers who came to meet him and they were anxious to show him something. They took him to a house overlooking a beach and pointed out to sea at a black boat some distance from the shore. "Quick," they said. "We must follow the black boat," and they dragged Bart with them out of the house and along the beach.

"No, I don't want to," said Bart, struggling to get free of them. Then he woke with a start and found himself tangled up in his sleeping bag.

He was relieved to find it was only a dream. He straightened himself out and tried to make himself comfortable. Maybe there's more to those birdwatchers than I thought, he mused. He tossed and turned and finally went back to sleep, but it wasn't until the early hours of the morning that his dreams became more gentle and he slept more soundly.

The next day, the others were up and about before Bart. Even Tom, who made a special effort.

Mrs B turned up with their breakfast at eight o'clock.

"Goodness me! The new boy still fast asleep? Well, I've brought an extra bowl and spoon, and extra toast.

Extra rations of everything in fact. I know what healthy appetites you have. Oh, and there are cheese and ham sandwiches in there as well, for later on. Now, do let me know if you need anything else. Anything at all."

As soon as she had gone, Tom and Shani ran off to check on the birdwatchers. Anna and Ian had decided this would be best, as they were less likely to be recognised.

The carriage was waiting by the hotel and Tom and Shani were just in time to see the birdwatchers climb aboard. They watched the carriage trundle off up the road and around the corner until it disappeared from view, then they trotted back to Base Camp to report their findings.

"They weren't carrying much," said Tom. "One of them had his camera and binoculars and the other was carrying a sort of briefcase."

"No suitcases then," said Ian. "Probably only going for the day."

"Well, at least we know our spies, special agent Kaz that is, will have them under surveillance," said Anna.

"Cor, it's exciting isn't it!" said Tom, rubbing his hands.

Bart finally woke up at this point. He heard the others chatting outside and remembered where he was. He smiled to himself. He was back with the Islanders and today they would be exploring Sark together. What could be better than that? He looked at his watch. Crikey! Quarter past eight. Better get a move on.

A few minutes later the door of Bart's tent opened and a slightly bleary Bart emerged. "Morning Bart," said the others. "Did you sleep well?"

"Not really," said Bart. "Had some really weird dreams."

"So did I," said Anna. "Come on, have some breakfast. You'll soon feel better. What did you dream about?"

Bart told them about his dream. "The funny thing was it felt like that house, and the beach and all that, it felt like I was in France."

"Well, you have just got back from France," said Ian.

"And sometimes when you dream everything gets mixed up," said Tom.

Bart nodded, but there was still something bothering him, about his dream.

"My mum says, when you dream, it's your brain sorting things out," said Tom. "You know, all of the things you've seen and done, it sorts them all out and puts them in the right compartments."

They finished breakfast and Ian took out the map of Sark so that they could plan their route.

"I'm going to take my sketch book," said Anna. "I haven't had nearly enough time for painting but I hope we'll find a few places where I can at least scribble off a quick sketch."

"So we're going right up north, are we?" said Bart. "Let's have a look."

The boys gathered around the map.

"The most northerly point would be the Bec du Nez," said Bart, pointing to a rock off the northern tip of Sark, "Or perhaps La Grune."

"But the map shows water between them and Sark," said Tom. "I'll just check on my chart." He dived into his tent and came out clutching the chart. "There you are," he said. "When it comes to rocks and depths of water, you can only get that from a good sea chart."

"You're right there, Tom," said Bart. "Look, it shows green all around those rocks, so that means it dries out at very low tides. Mind you, I'm not sure what it would be like, climbing over that lot."

"I think we should just go to where the path ends on the map and call that the north pole," said Ian. "It's always best to stick to the paths in Sark. Otherwise you might end up going back on the *Flying Christine** or worse. I wonder how we get into the caves though. It just says Boutiques (Caves) on the map, but the entrance could be anywhere."

"You never know. There might be a sign post," said Tom.

"I wouldn't bet on it," said Ian. "They don't seem to use signposts much over here."

"Fair enough," said Bart. "It wouldn't be much fun exploring if there were signposts for everything."

The girls had been dividing up the sandwiches and making ready to leave. They came over to see what the boys were up to.

"Have you seen the Avenue, Bart?" said Shani.

"Only once, years ago," said Bart.

"Perhaps we could pass through it on the way," said Anna, winking at Shani.

"Oh no, I know what you're up to," said Tom. "They want to go shopping again."

"Since it's quite an expedition you're planning," said

Anna, "We might need some special provisions."

"Ah no. Last time they were stuck in the shops for ages, Bart," said Tom.

"Well, as a matter of fact, there's somewhere I would like to look at on the way," said Bart, going back to the map. "I've never been to this place here, Point Chateau, and actually, if we went through the avenue and turned right at the end there, it wouldn't be that far. Would you mind?"

"I don't know if there would be time," said Ian. "It might be best if we did that first. It's near Bob's place, so we know the way there, and then we can do the avenue on the way to the pole."

"Good plan, Ian" said Bart. "It will be quicker that way round."

"We'd better make a start," said Ian. "We've a lot of ground to cover and it's a quarter past nine already."

"I wonder how Kaz is getting on," said Anna. "They must be on the boat by now."

They packed their bags with everything they thought they might need for the journey and set forth. They took the road across the Coupée and down into the wooded valley past Dixcart Hotel, where they looked for a path branching off towards Bob's cottage.

"The map shows a path leading off from the back of the hotel," said Ian.

They proceeded along the road, keeping a careful eye out for any sign of a likely path, but found nothing. They continued further, in the hope that something might turn up but the road narrowed and led off to the right.

"This is totally the wrong direction," said Ian.

Then Bart spotted a man working by the side of the road. He trotted over and asked the way to Point Chateau. The man took off his beret and scratched his head. "No, you're miles away," he said. "You'll have to go all the way back and head for the Avenue."

"What about the path around the back of the hotel?" said Ian, who had walked over with the map.

"I suppose you could go that way," said the man, "But it's a roundabout route." He thought for a moment. "Okay then," he said. "You go back along the path here until you see a pillar with an eagle on it. Turn right there and follow the path up the hill."

They thanked him and retraced their steps back to the hotel, where they found the eagle and took the path through the hotel grounds and up the other side of the valley. After a long hike uphill they eventually came to the top, and the Pomme de Chien campsite, then the path became more of a road which seemed to be leading them swiftly back to civilisation. They could see a row of buildings ahead of them.

"It certainly is a roundabout route," said Ian. "We're nearly back at the Avenue."

They turned a corner and saw a little red and grey tractor approaching. They kept to one side to allow it to pass, then, as it drew nearer, Anna said "It's Bob. Bob the boatman."

Bob was on his way down to his boat with a load of crab pots, ropes and floats in the link box attached to the back of the tractor. He waved, slowed down and stopped as he reached them. "Hello, you lot," he said, cheerily. "I've been hoping I might see you. How's it going? Found that buried treasure yet?"

The Islanders were still a little unsure of Bob, after the note he had sent them about the birdwatchers, and although they greeted him in a friendly fashion, he could sense a slight awkwardness in their manner. "I'm sorry I didn't have a chance to speak to you about those two men, you know, the Belgian gentlemen," he said. "It's a bit difficult to explain."

"You mean the birdwatchers?" said Anna.

"Oh no, they're not birdwatchers," said Bob. "Look, I'm sorry I can't say more about it. It's police business, you see. It's just better if you keep out of their way."

"That's okay, Bob," said Anna. "We haven't seen them for ages, anyway."

"Not since this morning!" Tom whispered to Shani.

"Good," said Bob. "So, what are you up to today?"

They explained where they were headed.

"Ah, Point Chateau. Yes, it's lovely out there. You need to follow this road, then take the first right and then there's a path on your left. Should be signposted. Good luck then. Have a nice day!"

Bob gave them a cheery wave, revved up the tractor and sped off towards the harbour.

"What was all that about?" asked Bart.

"Police business," said Tom.

"I bet it is police business too," said Anna. "I bet he knows they are a couple of crooks and he wants to catch them all by himself and take all the credit."

"Anna!" said Shani. "Let's not get too carried away with this. Remember what Kaz said about Bob. She said he was alright."

"Hmm," said Anna. "Mind you, he did seem pretty chummy with those two, Belgians, birdwatchers, whatever you want to call them, taking them out on his boat and all that."

"I don't get it," said Bart.

"Police business," Tom said again. "What about if they're all policemen?"

What, the birdwatchers?" said Anna.

"Yes," said Tom. "What about if the birdwatchers are policemen and they are working with Bob on something?"

"Something to do with the black boat," Ian suggested.

"Maybe," said Tom.

"Hey, in a funny kind of way that actually would make sense," said Anna. "But what on earth would two Belgian policemen be doing on Sark?"

Chapter 17

Kaz on a Special Mission

Inspector Jan Lomers and his assistant, Detective Sergeant Piet Van der Roost, had boarded the Sark Ferry *Le Bon Marin* and were sitting comfortably in the lower cabin while she ploughed her way across the Great Russel towards Guernsey. Now and then they spoke quietly to one another in Flemish and, as trained detectives of the Belgian police force (attached to Interpol) are bound to do, they looked about them, from time to time, at the other passengers. They needed to be aware of anything suspicious, of anything which might be connected in any way with their enquiries.

The beady eye of Inspector Lomers alighted on a sullen faced young girl sitting opposite. A pity, he thought to himself, she would be quite pretty if she did not look so stern, but where had he seen her before? The girl continued to read her book and did not look up. Ah, good, he thought, a chance to scrutinise some more. Had she been one of those children at the hotel? The ones who kept getting in the way? No, he did not think so.

Generally speaking, the two policemen had enjoyed their time on Sark. It was not often they were sent to such a beautiful place. The little cottage they had stayed in was so quaint, and their meals at the hotel had been excellent. Inspector Lomers had been quite smitten with the place and was planning to return. Perhaps he might take his wife for a short holiday. But the purpose of their visit this time had been to watch every move of the motor fishing vessel *Aurelie* of St Malo, and this task had not been made any easier by those infernal children popping up out of nowhere and making a proper nuisance of themselves each time he and his assistant had thought they might be getting close to something.

Ah well, perhaps he had been a little harsh with them. They were only children after all, playing their games, but it really had seemed to him at times as if he and the sergeant had been the ones under surveillance, rather than the crew of the black boat.

Anyway, their time on Sark had been well spent. They had not seen their suspects remove anything from the boat, and now the *Aurelie* had berthed in St Peter Port. If everything had gone to plan, Guernsey Customs would be searching the boat at this very minute and the Inspector was hopeful that they would find what they were looking for. All being well, he and Sergeant Van der Roost would soon be returning home, their mission successfully concluded.

Le Bon Marin rounded the Fourquies buoy and headed for the Tobars passage, around the southern tip of Jethou. Kaz was so familiar with the route that she hardly looked up from her book. Not that she was so completely engrossed in the story though. She could feel the gimlet eyes of one of the birdwatchers on her and she thought it best to try to avoid his gaze.

Perhaps the others were right about those two, she thought to herself. If they really were birdwatchers she would have expected them to be up on deck with their binoculars. There might be quite a few interesting birds to be seen on the rocks off Jethou.

"I'm going out for a smoke," said Sergeant Van der Roost to the Inspector, and he headed for the door, leaving the binoculars and camera behind.

Le Bon Marin threaded her way through the dog-leg passage and continued resolutely on her way towards Guernsey, the steady throb of her powerful diesel engines driving her determinedly on. She was quite a good old boat really, Kaz thought to herself, churning her way up and down, day in, day out, in virtually all weathers. It was only rarely, in the worst of the winter storms, a sailing might be cancelled.

Kaz continued to keep her head down and, before too long, they were approaching St Peter Port. The engines were throttled back as they passed through the pierheads and made their way to the jetty. The passengers started to gather their bags and make ready to leave. The crew made fast the mooring ropes and gathered by the exit door to help everyone step off.

Kaz waited for the birdwatchers to go first and then followed at a safe distance.

"Y'aright, Kaz?" said the friendly boatman helping her

off. "See y'again soon."

The long line of passengers leaving the boat filed up the steps and onto the jetty. Kaz was keeping a careful eye on the two men. They stopped by the waiting room. She stopped and pretended to adjust the handle of her suitcase. The thin one reached into his pocket, brought out a packet of small cigars and lit one up. They spoke briefly to one another and then headed off towards the passenger terminal on the New Jetty. Kaz followed at a sensible distance. She wondered if the men might be catching the next boat to St Malo or England. That would be the end of her job, if that were the case, and there would be nothing much to report back to the others, but no, they walked under the arch way, around the corner and up some steps onto the viewing area above the terminal building.

She carried on slowly behind them swinging her suitcase and trying to look as if she was dawdling aimlessly about the place, perhaps waiting to be collected. She arrived at the top of the steps. Out of the corner of her eye she could see the two men leaning on the parapet and looking over towards the pier by the harbour mouth. She wandered over to the other side and pretended to admire the view of St Peter Port, then she walked over to the end of the viewing area facing Castle Cornet. She glanced from time to time at the two men, but was extremely careful not to make it obvious. As she turned the corner and headed back towards them, she could see what they were looking at. Tied up alongside the pier was the object of their attentions, the black MFV *Aurelie* of St Malo, and it appeared that there was a great deal of activity onboard.

Kaz was still far enough away that the Belgians should not notice her. She leaned on the wall and pretended to look out to sea. There was certainly nothing suspicious in her behaviour as the view out over the top of the pier, of Herm and Jethou with Sark behind, would be attractive enough to anyone, but from this position she could see quite clearly what was happening on the *Aurelie*, and so could the two detectives.

Only one of the crew was visible and he was on deck having a heated discussion with two uniformed men. Probably Customs, thought Kaz. Then two more people in white shirts came up from below, one of them holding a dog on a leash. The crewman was joined by another and the discussion continued with raised voices and a great deal of shrugging and posturing and waving their arms on the part of the crew. The dog started barking and was dragged away. After a time things seemed to quieten down. Several Customs men left the boat, taking the dog with them, leaving one man who seemed to be checking the ship's papers.

For a moment, Kaz felt that one of the Belgians might be looking her way. She turned to face the castle again and then walked slowly back to her original position overlooking the town. Then she heard a ring tone and the shorter man answered his phone. He spoke briefly in English. "Yes … Nothing at all? … Very well … Yes, we will meet at your office in ten minutes."

He finished the call, said a few words in Flemish to his partner and then Kaz, who was still facing away from them, heard their footsteps approaching. She held her breath and could feel her heart thumping. At any moment, she imagined, a firm hand would grip her shoulder. But no, the footsteps turned away and the two men headed quickly down the stairway.

Kaz hesitated for a moment. She clutched her hand to her chest. At least she felt able to breath again. What now? she thought. She couldn't just run down the steps after them. They were going to someone's office. She had to find out where, and who it was they were meeting. These men were not birdwatchers at all. They were acting very suspiciously. The others were right, and they were depending on her. Well, she wouldn't let them down.

She grabbed her case and hurried quickly along the viewing area, looking down to see if she could spot the two men. Yes! There they were, walking briskly along the jetty. She ran as quickly as she could. She knew there was another way down at the inner end of the jetty.

The two men, by now, had left the jetty and were heading in towards the Town. Kaz found the staircase, rushed down and tried her best to catch them up. As she passed the shipping office she met the sailor who had helped her off the boat. "Do us a favour, Dave, will you," she panted, thrusting the suitcase at him. "Just stick that in the office for me. I'm off into Town for half an hour."

"Ah, shopping is it?" he replied with a grin. "Yeah, sure Kaz. Don't spend too much."

Kaz thanked him and ran off. The two men had disappeared but, as she reached the pedestrian crossing at the weighbridge, she caught sight of them on the other side of the road, walking towards a taxi rank. Oh no, not a taxi, she thought. She had no money for a taxi.

She crossed over on the next change of the traffic lights and was relieved to find that the men had turned left before the taxi rank and were heading up the hill. There were plenty of people milling about. This made it less likely she would be noticed but it was also possible she might lose them in the crowd. She tried to close the gap.

The men seemed to know where they were going. They turned left and marched briskly up a winding road towards the top of the town, then they turned right, through an archway in a high granite wall and into a courtyard with tall buildings on three sides. This was quite a surprise for Kaz. She looked up at the sign on the archway. 'Police Station.' If they were crooks, as the others thought they were, why would they be going into the police station?

She watched from the road as the two men strode purposefully up the steps and through the main entrance door. She waited for five minutes, then ten minutes, but there was no sign of them coming out. She looked at her watch. 11.30. She had better be getting back, but first she had to find a telephone box to phone the others.

The Islanders had found the path turning off to the left, as directed by Bob, at least, they thought it must be the one. They were beginning to realise that exploring in Sark can take longer than you think. Several times they had been confused by paths branching off this way and that way, with no signposts, leading to dead ends or doubtful routes over fields.

They arrived at a typical junction at the top of a valley, with three paths leading down, but this time there was at least a signpost to give them a clue.

"That one says 'To the bay,'" said Bart, "And that one says 'To the Hog's Back.'"

"That's the one we want," said Ian, but it looked like a short track leading up to a field gate.

"Let's give it a try, anyway," said Tom.

"We might have to go through the field," said Shani.

"Hey, look. There are some horses," said Tom. "I want to go and say hello."

They walked up the track and, as they reached the field gate, they found that it turned sharply to the right and led off towards the headland where they were hoping to find Point Chateau.

"This looks more hopeful," said Ian.

There were three piebald horses in the field which made the corner and they had gathered by the fence to meet the explorers. Tom went up and put out his hand to stroke one of the horses but it jumped back and snorted.

"That's not how you do it, Tom," said Shani. She put her hands behind her back and walked slowly up to the fence. She pursed her lips and blew out through her mouth, as one might blow on a candle flame to make it flicker.

The horse which had shied away eyed her suspiciously. She kept still and blew again. Slowly, the horse approached her and sniffed, its nostrils widening and twitching. After repeating this ritual several times, Shani and the horse were nose to nose.

"That's amazing, Shani," said Tom. "Where did you learn how to do that?"

"It's the animals' greeting," said Shani. "We spent the day on a farm once and the farmer showed us how to do it. It works on cows as well."

The others tried the greeting too, and although they did look strange, puffing and blowing, the horses seemed to like it and they all spent an enjoyable few minutes getting to know one another.

"I expect they must be carriage horses having the day off," said Anna. "They certainly look pretty sturdy. Strong enough to pull a carriage."

They said goodbye to the horses and trudged off along the path. As it progressed, the path became narrower and the vegetation on both sides became thicker and higher, in places arching over the top, then, as they came closer to the point, the sloe bushes thinned out and occasionally they caught a glimpse of the sea. Now, where few people ventured, the path was thickly carpeted with short cropped grass. They were moving almost silently along when suddenly something made them jump. They were stopped in their tracks. A loud beating of wings, like the sound of a helicopter, came out of nowhere, rising up beside them, close by, then whirring off and away.

"What on earth was that?" said Anna.

They looked around but could see nothing.

"A bird of some sort," said Bart. "Probably a pheasant breaking cover."

"I thought it was that helicopter again," said Shani.

"It didn't half make me jump," said Ian.

"Me too," said Tom. "Here, what time is it?"

"About a quarter past," said Ian.

"What, a quarter past eleven?" said Tom. "Cor, no wonder I was getting peckish. Come on, let's get to the point and stop for elevenses."

"Yeah, come on Tom, get to the point," said Ian.

The others joined in. "That's not the point! Oh, this is pointless! I can't see the point! No, the point is …"

Chapter 18

To Point Chateau and the North Pole

They continued on their way, laughing and joking, and soon reached the end of the path. Just before the end they had to negotiate a very narrow, crumbling part where the cliff fell away rapidly to their left, then they arrived on a small windswept plateau with a commanding view over all of the south east coast of Sark and out over a vast, silver, sparkling sea.

They were quiet for a moment while they took in the grandeur of the scene, then they went right out to the very end.

"Hey, look at this," said Bart. "I've found a cannon."

They gathered around the black barrel of a cannon, lying on the ground.

"There's writing on it," said Shani.

There was a crown and a monogram GR.

"That must be George Rex. Probably George the first," said Anna.

"There's a date here as well," said Bart. "I think it says 26-7-23. Or maybe that seven is a one."

"Must be George the first," said Anna. "That would make it 1723."

"Wow!" said Tom. "It's nearly three hundred years old. Well, it will make a jolly good seat for a picnic." He sat down on it and reached into his rucksack for a suitable snack.

"I wonder how Kaz is getting on," said Anna. "We haven't heard from her yet."

"I'm sure she'll phone soon," said Shani. "But she said she was being collected, didn't she? So maybe she'll phone us when she gets back home."

They made themselves comfortable on the wind flattened grass and heather of the hilltop, ate biscuits and fruit, and drank from their water bottles. Anna settled back against a rock and made some sketches. Tom identified some of the offshore reefs by looking at his sea chart.

"Straight ahead of us, that must be La Conchée. Right over there, to the left is Les Burons, and that one there, in the middle of the bay, just off Little Sark, that must be Baleine."

They were just thinking about leaving when Anna's phone went.

"That must be Kaz," she said excitedly. "Quiet everyone. Yes, hello. Hello Kaz. Yes … Yes … No, really? What, the black boat? It must have been Customs you reckon?" There was quite a long pause while Anna looked dumbfounded and they could hear Kaz talking at the other end. "No! So you actually saw them go in? And they were there for how long? Oh right … Right … Yes, Kaz. Well thanks ever so much. That's all really interesting … Yeah, we'll let you know if anything happens. Okay. Keep in touch then. Yep. Thanks again … Bye."

Anna switched off her phone and turned wide eyed to the others.

"You'll never guess what," she said and she went on to relate all that Kaz had told her.

"The police station?" said Shani. "Perhaps they realise the game is up and they've handed themselves in."

"Police business, remember?" said Tom. "That's what Bob said. I reckon I was right. Those birdwatchers are something to do with the police."

"This is getting more and more complicated," said Bart. "The birdwatchers from Belgium who might be crooks or they might be policemen, the black boat from France, searched by Customs, and they were all hanging around in Sark watching each other, and us watching them until Bob tells us not to."

"I know what we need," said Ian. "We need one of those blackboards or a notice board or something, like they have on TV. You know, where they write down all the evidence and stick on photos and things and it helps them to solve the crime."

"Anyone seen any blackboards around here?" said Tom.

"I know it's not the same, but we could do a miniature one with my sketch pad," said Anna. "I think that's a good idea, Ian."

So they all gathered around and took it in turns to

suggest what to put down, and Anna made little sketches to go with the words. In the end there were two pages of pictures in boxes, writing, crossing out, and arrows connecting some ideas to other ideas. They stood back and thought about it.

"I think we're getting closer," said Bart, "But there's still something missing."

"Yeah, but we've made a pretty good start," said Ian. "Well done, Anna. It looks just like the real thing."

"And we can add to it when something happens, or when we think of anything," said Shani.

"Right," said Ian, looking at his watch, "Good grief! It's nearly one o'clock. We'd better get a move on. We need to catch the low tide if we want to look at that cave."

"And we're going to show Bart the Avenue, don't forget," said Anna.

They hastily packed their things, took a last look at the view and set off in single file along the path. They soon reached the place where they had met Bob on his tractor and, shortly after, they found themselves on a road which led them past some quaint old granite cottages and then on to the end of the Avenue.

There was a fair amount of traffic in the Avenue: carriages, people on bicycles and holidaymakers browsing amongst the shops and cafés. Tom and Ian went into a book shop while Anna and Shani took Bart on a quick tour of the other shops. There were all sorts of interesting books and pictures in the book shop. Tom and Ian looked at a very old map of the Islands and chatted with the lady who ran the shop. They told her they were on their way to the Boutique Caves.

"Oooh," she said, "You know why they're called the Boutiques, don't you? It's because the smugglers used to keep their contraband in there before they sold it on. Yes, and did you know that Victor Hugo went to the Boutique Caves and he found a giant octopus* in there."

"What, a man eating octopus?" said Tom.

"Oh yes, that's what he claimed. I'm not sure about it but there are stories, you know, of fishermen having to fight them off."

"Cor, it's a good job I've brought my pen knife, Ian," said Tom. "I think I'll tie it to a stick and make a harpoon of it, just in case we meet one."

The boys were amazed at how many books had been written about Sark and how old some of them were. Sadly, their pocket money could not stretch to buying any, so they thanked the lady for helping them and went off to find the others. Having searched up and down the Avenue they eventually found them at the crossroads by the top of Harbour Hill.

"What kept you?" said Anna. "We've been waiting here for ages."

"Bet you haven't," said Tom.

"Anyway, we need to start from the other end and take that road past the Church," said Ian, looking at the map.

"Or we can take this one," said Bart, pointing up the road opposite, "And turn left at the end. That'll join up with the road we want."

They took the road Bart had suggested and started the long trek northward to the Pole. They were surprised at

the number of new buildings along the road and building
works in progress but, fairly soon, the buildings petered
out and they found themselves back in unspoilt countryside
with just the occasional house or bungalow along the
way.

"Aha, just the thing," said Tom reaching into a hedge
and pulling out a loose piece of bamboo. He explained
to the others about the giant octopus and how he might
have to fight it off with his harpoon.

"You are funny, Tom," laughed Shani.

"Yes, you can laugh, Shani," said Tom, "But you
might thank me later when you find yourself gripped in
its terrible, slimy tentacles. And then it will be Tom to the
rescue!" He acted out a sword fight against the octopus
with his bamboo, which made Shani laugh even more.

They followed the signs for Eperquerie Common,
passing the Seigneurie on the way, and in less than half an
hour they reached the end of the main road and followed
the path out across the common. They passed a turn off
on the right signposted 'To Fontaine Bay,' then another
to 'Landing and Bay,' but they ignored these and carried
straight on. The path, sheltered by sloe bushes and gorse
on both sides, led them, after several twists and turns,
across to the far end of the common and out onto a high
ledge, where they found another cannon and a bench on
which to sit and admire the view.

It had been quite a hike from the Avenue. Anna and
Shani plonked themselves down on the bench and the
boys sat down on the grass. Ahead of them, the path led
steeply down and then up again over the first of the three

pronounced humps leading out to the Bec du Nez, at the very northern tip of Sark.

"I haven't seen a sign for the Boutiques yet," said Tom.

"They must be somewhere around here, but it doesn't show exactly where on this map," said Ian. "Just a bit further, I reckon."

"Well, there's no way I'm going in, anyway," said Shani. "Not after the last time." She shuddered. "And especially not if there's a giant octopus lurking about." She laid back on the seat and pulled her hat down over her eyes. "I might as well stay here while the rest of you go," she said.

"Come on, Shani," said Anna. "You have to make it to the North Pole."

"Yes, come on, Shani," said Tom. "We can do that first, then you can wait for us while we go hunting for the octopus."

"Okay then," said Ian, getting to his feet, "Let's head for the Pole!"

The Islanders followed the narrow path which took them steeply down and then up over the first hill. Looking down to their left, they were surprised to see two people sitting on some rocks at the base of the cliffs.

"How did they get down there?" said Tom. "Do you think that's the Boutiques, Ian?"

"It can't be," said Ian. "Not according to the map."

They continued over the top and down again to face a second hill. Between the two hills was a huge cleft, about 4 metres wide, with sheer sides dropping down to a rocky floor. They skirted round it and headed up the second hill where they could see the remains of a granite tower perched on top. At times now it was more like climbing than walking. They had to balance and leap from rock to rock like mountain goats. They reached the summit and stopped to explore the tower, about half of which was still standing, with various crumbling granite walls and stone floors around and about it.

"It must have been a tiny fortress," said Shani.

"A lookout tower," said Anna.

"Just look at the view all around from here," said Ian. "You'd see the enemy approaching from just about anywhere."

"Come to think of it," said Bart. "I'm pretty sure the caves must be more or less under this tower somewhere. I'm sure I remember seeing some caves when we came by boat, and if you looked up you could see this tower almost directly above them."

Tom was sitting on one of the low walls carefully finishing off the harpoon. "Aha. So we must be getting closer," he said.

From the lookout tower they could see the path leading down to the most northerly point of Sark. Beyond this the slope broke off into a channel, strewn with rocks and boulders, which, at high tide, would separate Sark from the final hump of La Grune.

"We might as well call this the North Pole," said Bart. "What do you think?"

They thought about it and decided that the tower marked the spot pretty well. It may not have been quite as far north as they could go but somehow it just felt right. So they held the customary ceremony to mark the occasion, shook hands, and Anna wrote a note on a scrap of paper from her sketch book: 'Islanders Expedition to North Pole of Sark. August 2009.' which they all signed, and she pushed it under a loose stone in the wall.

"It's going to be quite a long walk back," said Bart. "If we're going to find these caves we'd better get a move on."

"I'm ready," said Tom, brandishing his harpoon above his head. "Ready to face the octopus!"

"I shall make my way back to the seat by the cannon," said Shani, disapprovingly, "And wait for you there."

"Here, Shani. Take my phone," said Anna. "You can be look-out. Phone Bart on his phone if you see anyone else coming down."

Bart made sure his phone was switched on.

Ian suggested that they may as well carry on down to the very end of the path and see if that led them to the caves. They threaded their way carefully down the hill and soon found themselves on a rocky foreshore. They searched around to the right and the left. It took some time but finally it was Bart who found the entrance.

"Over here! Over here!" he shouted in great excitement. "This must be it."

They gathered around and peered into the darkness of the cave. As their eyes grew slowly accustomed to it they edged inside and stood and stared in amazement.

Chapter 19

The Giant Octopus of the Boutique Caves

Clearly, the entrance they had found would be underwater at certain times as the floor and sides of the cave were still wet and shiny. Their first obstacle was a mound of seaweed washed in by the tide, but beyond that they could see a long tunnel funnelling out, becoming taller and wider as it stretched out before them. At the far end a mysterious light filtered through, delicately playing on the dark and soaring arches of a vast internal cavern.

Tom charged at the seaweed and plunged his harpoon deep into its side. "Take that, you horrible sticky monster!" he shouted. His words rose up and echoed about the cave, bouncing back at them. The others laughed and their laughter too echoed about the place, then they were silent, in awe of the forces of nature which had created this place. They edged cautiously past the seaweed and made their way slowly and carefully amongst the pools and puddles of the stony floor, working their way deeper and deeper in towards the inner sanctum.

They felt their way along, Ian lighting the way with a torch. Gradually they could see more. The tunnel continued along for some 50 to 60 paces, then the light shone in quite brightly from the right and they could see clearly before them a huge central chamber with a great square natural window in its side, facing out to sea. They no longer needed torches at this stage and were able to clamber out across flat sections of rock to peer out of the window.

It was then that Bart thought he might have heard something. A low babble, then the sound of footsteps, pebbles scrunching underfoot.

"I can hear voices!" he whispered.

The others stopped and listened intently but there was nothing.

"Don't be silly Bart," said Anna. "You're just imagining it. Anyway, Shani would have phoned if she had seen anyone."

"There's no one here, Bart, only us, and one dead octopus of course." said Tom.

Bart listened again, cupping his hand to his ear.

The others walked slowly back inside.

"The size of this place!" whispered Ian. "I wasn't expecting anything so big."

"Can't you just imagine the smugglers?" said Anna. "Isn't it awesome?"

"Perfect for unloading stuff from a boat," said Ian, "And there's all this space. It's like a huge warehouse."

They were whispering amongst themselves and Bart

had just rejoined them when, suddenly, a powerful beam of light shone down on them and a voice boomed out: "Oi! You lot. What do you think you're doing in here?"

The Islanders were dazzled by the light which was shining down from the inner part of the cave where it diminishing again in size to form a second tunnel, and rose up steeply to what appeared to be another entrance or exit. They tried to shield their eyes and could just make out three dark shapes silhouetted against the daylight filtering through.

"Well? What have you got to say for yourselves?" said the first shape, a rather stout and stern sounding woman.

"Er, we're just having a look around," ventured Anna.

"Oh, just having a look around is it?" said the woman. "Well I wonder whether your parents know what you're up to. Don't you realise how dangerous it is to just have a look around in these caves?" She looked at her watch. "It's well past low tide. Another half an hour and you could be swimming for it."

The Islanders felt terribly embarrassed. They had not realised they were doing anything wrong.

The spotlight was taken off them and shone around the cave. The woman spoke to the people behind her, then they climbed carefully down the slope towards the children. It was now possible to see them more clearly. The woman was wearing a climber's helmet and had a coil of rope over her shoulder.

"Well this is a fine state of affairs," she said to the Islanders, who were still lost for words. "Next time you decide to go caving, for goodness sake make sure you do it properly." She fished about in her pockets. "Here. This is my card. Now you just wait here for five minutes, while I finish off, and I'll take you out with me."

The Islanders could see there was no point in arguing with this person. Perhaps they had been wrong to venture into the cave. They stood sheepishly in a huddle and waited while she completed her tour, pointing out the various features of the cave to her group. Ian shone his torch on the card so the others could read it: ' Rocks and Hard Places. Gillian Prendergast's Guided Tours of Sark. The Caves and Shoreline. Historical walks.'

Five minutes later they were being herded up towards the exit. They walked towards the light and, climbing up, they found themselves on a threshold, in bright sunshine, looking down a rubble strewn slope to the shoreline.

"Careful now!" boomed Gillian Prendergast.

They scrambled down and looked about them to find their bearings.

"Where are we?" said Anna.

"Hang on," said Bart. "Look over there. Isn't that the gorge that we saw from the top?"

Mrs Prendergast looked at them disapprovingly. "You just follow me," she said.

They clambered over the rocks and could now see, at the end of the gorge, a steep path snaking up to the cliff top above. It was not the easiest of paths to climb. Mrs Prendergast went on ahead, paying out the rope behind her. When she reached the top she barked out the order for them to follow, one at a time.

Tom was next up after Anna, followed by Ian and Bart, then the couple on the guided tour. It was certainly easier with the help of the rope than it would have been without it.

Soon they were all gathered at the top in the sunshine. The Islanders thanked Mrs Prendergast for showing them the way.

"That's alright, kids," she said, coiling her rope and placing it over her shoulder. "Now, do be careful won't you. We have enough accidents around here, you know. People straying off the paths, caught out by the tides, all that sort of thing."

They let the guided tour go ahead of them and followed on behind over the top of the hill from where they could see Shani waiting for them on the bench.

Shani had enjoyed her time on look-out duty. She had happily settled herself down on the bench by the cannon to keep watch. She thought about the others down in the cave and shuddered. There was no way she wanted to be down there with them. The weather seemed to be changing again. A little breeze had picked up and the sky was gradually clearing.

It was so lovely to be out in the fresh air. The sun was shining through the clouds with greater strength, lighting up the scene around her, brightening the colours of the sea, the sky, the white weathered craggy rocks of the hill tops leading out to the point and the greens, pinks and purples of the plant life clinging to the slopes.

She took off her hat, put her head back and allowed the

sun to warm her. As it brightened and faded she watched, through closed eyes, the colours changing from yellow to orange to red and back. The air, she noticed, smelt so clean and fresh and lightly scented by the wild flowers. She listened and could hear the waves breaking on the rocks below, the seagulls squawking and, somewhere from above, high in the sky, was that a skylark?

This certainly beats London, she thought to herself. What a shame they would soon be going back. There hadn't been enough time, really, just to enjoy the place, let alone explore it properly. Then she thought about her family. She missed her mother, and her father, and perhaps even her brothers too, but then again, she wouldn't have missed out on this trip with the Islanders, not for the world.

She reached this happy conclusion, then allowed her thoughts to wander off in other directions. She felt warm and comfortable and it was not very long before she drifted off and fell asleep.

Perhaps fifteen minutes passed, and she would probably have continued to sleep if she had not been disturbed.

"Hello," came a voice into her head.

"Hello!"

She woke with a start and looked up to see a middle-aged couple looking down at her.

"Oh, I'm sorry. Did we wake you?" said the woman. "Are you here all by yourself?"

"No, yes … no," said Shani, rubbing her eyes. Oh my goodness, she thought. What kind of a look-out have I been? "No, I'm waiting for my friends," she said finally.

"Oh, right," said the woman, with a kindly smile. She spoke with an American accent. "We were just wondering if the path continues on to the end."

"Sort of," said Shani, "But it isn't the easiest of paths."

"Uhuh," said the woman. She nodded and turned to her husband. "Looks like this is the end of the line, sugar."

They wished Shani to have a nice day and set off back across the common.

Shani looked at her watch. Oh dear, she thought, I must have drifted off. Better try harder. No good falling asleep on look-out duty. She sat up and looked around her. No sign of the others yet. Then she looked out to sea. In the distance, out towards Jethou, she thought she could see a boat approaching. The sun was reflecting off the water, turning it to bright shining gold. She shielded her eyes and looked again. Yes, it was definitely coming this way, probably the ferry, she thought. She wondered if perhaps the birdwatchers were on it, returning from their day in Guernsey.

Another ten minutes passed. The boat, which now she could see clearly was the Sark ferry, reached the point off Bec du Nez, and she watched as it passed quite close inshore, heading around towards the harbour.

She looked at her watch again. They had been gone nearly an hour now. Then she heard voices and, shortly after, a group of people appeared on the hilltop in front of her, marching down and then up towards her, but it was not the Islanders. It was a group of rock climbers, by the look of it, led by a stout woman wearing a helmet, with a rope coiled over her shoulder. She fixed Shani with a withering look as she reached the plateau. "Well, thank goodness at least one of you has some sense," she said, and strode off with the others following in her wake, leaving Shani without a clue as to what she was talking about. Minutes later there was a shout and the Islanders appeared and waved.

"What was all that about?" said Shani, as the others reached her.

"What, who, her?" said Anna. "Yes, she completely ruined our exploring in the cave."

"Yeah, gave us the third degree. You know, interrogation, shone a light on us and everything," said Bart.

"She was right though," said Ian. "We wouldn't have gone on our own if we had known."

"It's a really enormous cave, Shani," said Tom.

"Oh really, Tom? And did you find the giant octopus?"

"First thing I did," said Tom. He raised his harpoon

and acted out the story. "He was hiding under a heap of seaweed but I didn't give him a chance. With my trusty harpoon I struck and struck again until he was no more!"

"Tom, you are a complete nutter," said Anna, but they all laughed.

Tom continued his imaginary fight with the octopus. "Ah yes, you may laugh," he said, "At my Tom-foolery."

They all burst out laughing again.

"Oh, that's very good, Tom," said Shani. "Tom-foolery."

"Still, at least we made it to the North Pole," said Bart.

"And we did get to see most of the cave," said Ian, "And we discovered it by ourselves."

"Hang on, Shani," said Anna. "How come you didn't raise the alarm? You must have seen those people. They must have walked right past you."

Shani felt herself blushing.

"I don't know how they got down there. I didn't see them," she said.

Tom looked at Shani. "Maybe they were the people we saw on the rocks earlier on," he said. "Maybe you can get around to it that way."

"I did see the ferry come across," said Shani. "I was thinking how the birdwatchers might be on it."

"Do you think we should carry on calling them birdwatchers," said Tom, "Even if we know they aren't."

"Trouble is, we don't know, for sure, what they are," said Anna.

Chapter 20

The Birdwatchers Return

As time was getting on they decided to go back by the shortest route along the main roads. They crossed the common and marched off down the long straight road past the Seigneurie.

"So, what are we going to do tomorrow?" said Anna. "What would you like to do, Bart?"

"Would you like to see the Pilcher Monument?" said Shani. "It's terribly sad though."

"No, I've seen the monument before," said Bart. "We've landed there a few times by boat."

"What about a swim?" said Tom. "If it's nice we could go to Dixcart."

"That would be great," said Bart, "But I'd like to have a look at that secret cave if it's possible."

"Of course it's possible," said Anna. "We know the way down to it, don't we Shani? At least we'd have the place to ourselves. Kaz said hardly anyone knows about it."

"Okay, that's settled then," said Ian. "I'd like to see

it too."

Less than an hour later, they were approaching La Coupée when they heard the rumble of carriage wheels behind them. They stood to one side to allow the carriage to pass. It was the carriage that Tom and Shani had seen earlier that day, returning to the Sablonnerie. The driver gave them a cheery wave but the two passengers looked very serious and hardly acknowledged them.

"The birdwatchers!" said Anna in a hoarse whisper as they trundled past.

"There, I was right," said Shani, once they were out of earshot. "They probably were on that ferry. They've come back."

"But why?" said Tom. "The black boat must still be in Guernsey. Why would they come back here?"

"There's something we've missed," said Bart. "It doesn't make sense."

"When we get back, I think we should have another look at the blackboard," said Anna.

They walked slowly, to allow the birdwatchers to get well ahead. They did not want them to think they were being followed.

By the time they reached the Coupée, the carriage had crossed over and the birdwatchers were leaning on the railings, looking over towards Guernsey.

The Islanders held back and waited. They pretended to admire the view from the raised bank where they had spied on the birdwatchers before. The others sat or stood around while Ian laid himself down and peered at the two men through his telescope. "They're looking at a map, or something, and pointing over towards the Fontaine," he said. "Looks like the carriage has gone on ahead, now they're putting the map away, or it could be a sea chart. Now they're moving off again, heading towards Little Sark."

"Come on then," said Tom, "Let's follow them."

They waited till the birdwatchers had crossed over and disappeared from view, then they galloped down from the bank and crossed over themselves. On reaching Little Sark they carried on as quietly as they could up the hill, watching and listening for any sign of the two men.

They reached a corner where the roadside hedges were thick and high. They could see nothing but could hear voices speaking in a foreign language. They stopped.

"It must be them," whispered Anna. She crept to the corner and sneaked a quick peep, then she crept back again. "They're just around the corner, standing by a field gate."

They heard the gate click and the hinges groan as it was opened and closed again. The voices slowly faded away.

"They must have gone into the field," said Anna. "Hang on. I'll have a quick look."

She crept up to the corner, looked around, and motioned them to follow her. They reached the field gate and stopped again, under cover of the hedge, while Anna looked for the men. "They're at the other end of the field now, climbing over a stile," she said.

"Isn't this the gateway we need to take to get to the secret cave?" said Shani.

"I think you could be right, Shani," said Anna. "Kaz said there was a stile. I hope they're not going to find the way down. That would spoil everything."

"Do you think we should follow them?" said Tom.

"I think we're getting a bit too close for comfort," said Ian. "You know what they can be like. They can be pretty nasty if they think they're being spied on."

"Tell you what," said Bart. "They probably wouldn't recognise me, and if I go down the other side of the hedge they probably won't see me anyway."

"Okay," said Anna. "It's worth a try."

Bart ran along to the next field gate, hopped over it, doubled back and then headed out in the same direction as the birdwatchers, but on the other side of the hedge. He slowed down as soon as he heard voices and crept forward as quietly as he could.

The birdwatchers now had reached the corner of the field where Anna had tied a piece of string to the fence to mark the way down. Bart found a tiny gap in the hedge where he could just about see them. They were talking and pointing out over the cliff top, then they examined their map and searched up and down along the fence looking for a way through. The thinner man raised his arms and shrugged. He said something in Flemish, took out his cigars and lit one up.

The larger man seemed to agree with him, then took out his mobile phone and dialled a number. He put the phone to his ear, then started to talk in English. Bart listened intently.

"Bob?" said the man. "Yes, vee haf a problem. We

think we have found it but there is no way down … Yes … Yes, we must go there by boat … It is too late now, Bob? Okay, maybe tomorrow … as soon as you can make it then … Same place as last time? … Okay, bye."

Sensing that the birdwatchers were about to leave, Bart crept away and then ran as fast as he could back to the others. They were waiting by the gateway of the second field. "Well, Bart? How did it go?"

"Come on," said Bart. "We'd better get clear first. They're on their way back."

They set off at a good trot down the road and did not stop until they reached the hotel. Then Bart told them what he had seen and heard.

"Sounds like they were trying to find a way down," said Anna.

"Do you think it was Bob the boatman they were phoning?" said Shani.

"More than likely," said Anna. "They mentioned a boat and we've already seen them out once with Bob."

There was no time to go over the clues in Anna's sketch book. They were running late and had to smarten themselves up for dinner.

There was no sign of the birdwatchers in the restaurant that evening, but Mr Riley was on top form, entertaining them with snippets of information gleaned from the locals and interesting stories about Sark's past.

After dinner they returned to Base Camp and discussed their plans for the next day.

"If the birdwatchers are trying to find the secret cave, I think we should jolly well get there first," said Anna. "I'm sure Kaz wouldn't want just anybody tramping about the place."

"I suppose if we got there first they couldn't really say anything much about it," said Ian. "It's not as if it's a private beach or anything like that."

"Yes, we'd have just as much right to be there as anyone," said Tom.

"More, in fact," said Anna.

They settled down in their tents and tried to go to sleep. Tom drifted off more or less straight away, and so did Shani, but the other three were thinking about all that had happened and trying to make sense of it.

Ian just lay there perplexed by it all. Was it really as exciting as the others made out? The birdwatchers could just be people on holiday. They might have walked through the fields to look at the view, or maybe they were looking for a particular bird. Yes, Kaz had seen them in Guernsey at the harbour, but perhaps they were just enjoying looking at the boats. Okay, the visit to the police station was odd but there might be a simple explanation for it.

Bart too was perplexed. It was all too complicated, and he really preferred to put things down on paper. It was usually easier that way to make sense of things. The black boat, the birdwatchers, the boat being searched in Guernsey, what had they been looking for? It could have been a routine search by Customs of course. But he did think somehow they were all connected. He would have to look at Anna's sketch book in the morning. That would be better. Hopefully he would be fresher in the morning after a good night's sleep.

Anna had taken things a step further. She had taken out her sketch book and, turning away from Shani, so as not to disturb her, she pulled her sleeping bag over her head and shone her torch on the pages where she had set out all of the events which had taken place.

The old lady at Cliff Cottage: no, that was nothing to do with it. She crossed her out.

The birdwatchers: they were from Holland or Belgium, and they were connected in some way with the black boat. They might be policemen or they might be crooks.

The black boat: that was from France. It was flying the French flag anyway.

No, going back to the birdwatchers, she thought they must be policemen because they were in contact with Bob and they had visited the police station in Guernsey. Plain clothes though, so they could be detectives.

So, what if there were some Belgian detectives following a French boat, and the boat was searched in Guernsey and they found nothing. Ah, but the boat had been to Sark first. What if they had hidden something on Sark? That could be why the birdwatchers (or more likely detectives) had come back. Whatever it was they had been looking for, if there was nothing on the boat in Guernsey, they must have left it in Sark. But Bart thought there was something else, something missing?

By this time, the others had all fallen asleep, but Anna continued to rack her brains. She did not feel at all tired. She had found a pencil and was scribbling feverishly on the pages, crossing things out and adding new words here and there.

The French cigarette packet: they had forgotten about that. Something else to do with France, but who had left it there and what were they up to? The Belgians smoke cigars, so it wasn't them. Could it have been the people from the black boat? Yes, they could have landed by the secret cave. Then it struck her. She shrieked.

"What? What on earth - ?" said Shani, suddenly sitting bolt upright.

"I've got it! I've got it!" said Anna.

"Oh, not now, Anna, please. I want to go to sleep."

"But, Shani, I've got it. I've solved the mystery. I know exactly what's going on."

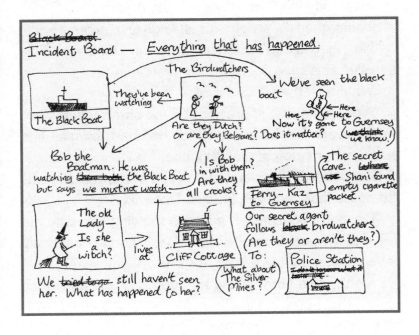

Bart and Ian had been woken. Seeing Anna and Shani's tent all lit up and, hearing voices, they scrambled out of bed grabbed a jumper and rushed over. Tom half woke up briefly but then turned on his side and went back to sleep.

"What's up? What's up?" said the boys. They wondered what was happening. Had the girls been attacked or something?

Anna opened the door. "I've worked it out!" she said. "Come in, come in. Sit down. Listen!" She was just so excited. "I don't know why we didn't see it before. It's so obvious!"

"Calm down, Anna," said Shani. "For goodness sake calm down and tell us what this is all about."

"It's to do with Bart's dream," said Anna.

Shani sighed. "Oh right. It's all to do with dreams is it?"

"No, no, you don't understand, Shani. This is real. This is really happening."

"What is it, then?" said Bart.

"Well, you said you dreamt that the birdwatchers were on the beach by the house which had been burgled and they were pointing at the black boat."

Bart nodded in agreement. "Well, I'm not sure if it was the house that had been burgled," he said.

"But don't you see? They were showing you who did it. It was the people on the black boat. That was how they got away, on the black boat. It's French, you see?"

"Right," said Ian, rubbing his eyes, "So you think they robbed that house on the French coast and then escaped here?"

"I suppose it makes sense," said Bart.

"Of course it makes sense!" said Anna. "Everything

fits into place. The birdwatchers are detectives. They've probably been chasing this gang across Europe. Then the baddies need somewhere to stash their loot. Where better than Sark, with all of its caves and nooks and crannies? But the detectives get wind of it and follow them over here. That's why they were watching them, to see if they unloaded the stuff. But they didn't see them do it, so they reckoned it must still be on the boat. That's why they had Customs search it when it put into Guernsey."

"That's amazing," said Bart. "Why didn't I think of that?"

"So now, if it wasn't on the boat, they probably left it here," said Ian.

"Absolutely," said Anna, "And I think I know where, don't you?"

"The secret cave?" said Shani.

"I think it must be," said Anna. "It's probably the only place where the detectives couldn't see them from the cliffs. And there's the empty cigarette packet too. French, you see, and someone dropped it right by the entrance to the cave."

"So, what are we going to do?" said Ian.

"They must have hidden the jewels in the cave," said Anna.

"It would be too dangerous to go down now, in the dark," said Shani.

"There could be hundreds of thousands of pounds worth," said Bart.

"It'll have to be first thing in the morning," said Anna, "And we'd better take a spade."

Chapter 21

Digging for Buried Treasure

There had been so much excitement during the night that most of the Islanders had slept badly and at 7 o'clock, although some were awake, nobody felt quite ready to leap out of bed and get on with the day. Even Anna, who was normally ready to go at the crack of dawn, was not feeling as bright and breezy as usual. What if she had been wrong? What if there was nothing in the cave? It had been guess work after all. She mulled it over in her mind, took out her sketch pad, checked over the scribblings of the previous night and, gradually, as the pieces of the puzzle fitted into place, she started to feel more confident again. She looked over at Shani, who was still dozing. I bet Tom is still asleep as well, she thought, and he doesn't even know what's in store for him today. This could be the most exciting part of their adventures yet. She looked at her watch. Nearly 7.30. High time we got started, she thought. She reached over and prodded Shani.

Ian had been going through a similar routine with Tom.

He was dying to tell Tom about Anna's ideas but he knew there was no point in waking him too early. It would go in one ear and out the other. Tom just didn't seem to be able to operate before 8 o'clock. Well, that's too bad, thought Ian, it's half past seven and I can't wait any longer.

Bart, who had actually slept better than he expected to, was woken by a shout from Tom and Ian's tent.

"No! That's incredible," shouted Tom. "Why didn't you wake me up last night, Ian? Cor, that's amazing. They could be like international jewel thieves. Blimey, we'd better get down there as quick as we can. Straight after breakfast, anyway."

The Islanders were soon up and breakfasted. Anna borrowed a spade from Mrs B. "Digging for buried treasure, is it?" she said with a knowing look.

"Something like that," said Anna. "We'll be careful to put things back as we find them though. We won't make a mess."

The weather seemed to be shaping up nicely. There was hardly any wind, the skies were clear and the sun was shining. They took packed lunches and their swimming things, thinking that, if they did not find any hidden treasure they might as well make a day of it. There was a spring in their step as they marched along the road. They were excited, not knowing exactly what might happen, but there was the prospect of finding stolen jewels and solving a crime. There was an element of danger too but they tried to put this at the back of their minds.

They reached the gateway, undid the gate and filed through into the field, carefully closing the gate behind them. They looked around to make sure nobody was watching, trotted along the edge of the field and climbed over the stile at the end. Once they were in the second field they felt a little more relaxed as they could no longer be seen from the road. They made their way down to the end and found Anna's piece of string tied to the fence.

"This is the place," said Anna.

"Cor, it doesn't look like it," said Tom. "No one would think there was a way down from here."

"You just follow me," said Anna, pushing down on the fence and stepping carefully over it. They all followed, one at a time, squeezed through the bushes on the other side and found themselves on the headland above the bay. Anna led them along a very narrow and difficult, winding path leading down to the rocky ledge cut into the cliff face, then down again over the boulders, up over a large black rock and finally down the other side and onto the beach. All was quiet around them, only the sound of the waves breaking gently on the sand. They looked out to sea but there was not a boat to be seen. They had the place entirely to themselves.

"This is amazing," said Bart. "What a lovely little bay and it's not on the map or anything."

"You just wouldn't know it was here," said Ian.

Anna and Shani smiled and nodded, pleased that the boys were impressed.

"You wait till you see the cave," said Anna.

She led them up the same way that Kaz had shown them, so that they could not see the entrance to the cave until she pointed it out.

"Wow," said Ian, "It really is a secret cave."

They made ready to go inside, all except for Shani who was really not too keen. "I'll keep watch out here," she said.

"Well mind you do," said Anna. "We don't want those birdwatchers sneaking up on us. Here take my phone."

"It might not work though, when you're in the cave," said Shani.

"In that case, you'll just have to stick your head in and shout," said Anna.

"Come on then," said Tom, who was dying to see inside. "We've got buried treasure to find. Ahaar me hearties! Gold dubloons and pieces of eight!"

It was pitch black inside the cave, darker than Anna had remembered it. They couldn't see a thing without their torches. She shone hers ahead and led them along the passage leading to the inner chamber. Half way along, she showed them the narrow slit leading to the second passage. "That one goes back down to the water's edge," she said.

"Cool," said Bart. "Can you actually get through though? It must be really tight."

"Just about," said Anna.

They reach the inner cavern and carefully shone their torches all around to see if there was any sign of buried treasure.

"If it's buried, it must be in here," said Tom. "It's too rocky in the other part but it's nice and sandy here, and it's dry too."

"It might not be buried," said Ian. "It might be stuck in

a hole in the wall, or something like that."

They could not see anything in the walls of the cave so they decided to start digging up the sand.

"Shall we start in the middle?" said Tom, holding the spade ready, "Or shall we start at one end and work our way across?"

"Let's start at the far end," said Anna, "And work our way back to the tunnel."

"Okay," said Tom. He started with great gusto, shovelling the sand, but soon hit solid rock. "It's really shallow over here," he said. "I'm going to try over there." He moved to another part of the cave and started digging as hard as he could, but he found it hard to make an impression. The sand was so dry that, as soon as he dug a hole, it filled in again from the sides. "Oh, this is hopeless," he said, but just then the spade hit something solid. He tossed the spade aside, got down on all fours and scraped frantically with his hands. "This could be it!" he exclaimed. "Come on lads, give us a hand." Bart and Ian joined him, but their excitement soon turned to disappointment when they unearthed a large piece of granite.

Tom carried on digging for a while in other parts of the cave but all he found were more stones.

"Sorry boys, this might not be as easy as we thought," said Anna.

Bart took a turn and so did Ian. By this time they had dug up about half of the floor and still had not found anything. Anna was beginning to think perhaps she had been wrong. It was her turn to dig next. She tried the very centre of the cave, plunged the spade in and, sure enough, hit something solid, but again, as they scraped away the sand, they found only a large flat stone.

"This is no good," said Anna. "Surely it must be here somewhere."

She was wondering where to try next when they heard a shout.

"Hey! Somebody! Come quickly!"

It was Shani.

"Tom, you'd better go and see what the trouble is," said Anna.

"It's okay, I'll go," said Ian, and he found his way quickly to the entrance.

As soon as he emerged Shani grabbed him and pointed out to sea.

"Wait a minute, Shani," said Ian, blinded by the bright sunlight. He shielded his eyes and peered out as best he could in the direction she was pointing. Then he saw what the problem was. "Oh no, blast!" he said, and ducked down out of sight.

"It's the black boat," hissed Shani.

"Heading this way," said Ian. "Hang on, Shani, I'd better tell the others. Wait here."

Ian rushed back inside. "Stop everything," he said, "It's the black boat. It's coming into the bay."

"Oh, crumbs," said Bart. "Now we're for it. What can we do?"

"Quick, start shovelling the sand back, just in case," said Anna. "I'll go and see how close they are."

"Maybe they're just passing by," said Tom.

"I don't think so," said Ian.

Tom and Ian helped Bart to scrape back all of the sand they had dug out then they trod it down, trying to make it look as if it had not been disturbed. After a minute or two Anna rushed back. "We've had it," she said. "They've anchored just offshore. There's no way we can get away without them seeing us."

"Oh no," said Bart. "There must be something we can do. But they haven't come ashore yet. We don't know for certain they are coming to the cave."

"I'm pretty sure they will be," said Anna.

Perhaps we should just make a run for it," said Ian. "While there's still time."

"Wait a minute," said Tom. "What about the other cave? The one that joins up with this one?"

"What about it?" said Anna.

"If we can all squeeze through, we can hide in there till they've gone."

"Yes, but what about Shani?" said Anna.

"It's our only hope," said Ian.

"Okay," said Anna, "We'll have to move fast. You and Bart go in now, Ian. Tom and I will try and get Shani in."

Ian and Bart had a last look around and smoothed off the sandy floor as best they could. They made sure they had left nothing behind and found their way through the narrow crack into the second tunnel, where they waited for the others.

Tom and Anna had gone out to fetch Shani who was hiding behind the rocks at the entrance to the cave, watching the black boat. They joined her and watched as the crew launched their rubber dinghy and climbed down into it.

Chapter 22

All is Revealed

"Shani, you must come with us," said Anna. "We're going to hide in the other tunnel. It's our only chance."

"No, I can't do it," said Shani, almost crying. "I can't go into that cave. I'd rather give myself up."

"You can't do that, Shani," said Tom. "You might get killed. They probably have guns. They might shoot you."

"I can't do it, I can't," said Shani.

"Come on. You have to, Shani," said Anna. "We're not going without you."

"No, you must go," said Shani. "Please go, and leave me here."

Tom put his arm around her. "Come on, Shani. It'll be alright. We'll hold your hand. Anna will lead the way and I'll be right behind you."

The men in the rubber dinghy were half way to the beach. There was no doubt now where they were headed. Tom noticed that one of them carried a spade.

Shani was shivering with fear, not so much fear of the

men from the black boat as fear of entering the cave, of being swallowed up in the darkness and suffocated by the terrible forces pressing in on her.

The men were getting closer. Now they had nearly reached the shore.

Shani's mind was in turmoil. She had tried so hard to overcome her fear but she just felt sick and helpless. She was terrified of going back into the cave, but then, suddenly, a thought flashed into her head which somehow brought her the briefest moment of calm and a glimmer of hope. She thought of the others, the Islanders, how she was one of them and how she couldn't let them down.

"Okay, I'll do it," said Shani.

"Thank goodness for that," said Anna, "Come on then, there's no time to waste."

"Well done, Shani," said Tom. "That's really brave of you. Now take a few deep breaths. I'll be right behind you."

The dinghy had landed on the beach and the men were pulling it clear of the water as Tom and Anna led Shani into the cave. They held hands and felt their way along until they reached the narrow gap leading through to the other cave.

"Nearly there, Shani," whispered Anna. "We just have to squeeze through here."

Shani felt the cold hard rock touching her back and front. "No, I can't," she whimpered, but she forced herself to go on.

"Well done, Shani," whispered Tom. "You're doing fine, we're nearly there."

Just as they finally squeezed through, they heard voices speaking in French and scrunching of boots on pebbles at the entrance to the first cave.

"Our rucksacks?" whispered Anna.

"It's alright, we've got them," Bart whispered back.

Shani was comforted to some extent to be back with the others. There was some relief at having escaped the clutches of the men from the black boat, even though they might yet be discovered. She also took some comfort that there was at least daylight at the end of this tunnel, where it led out onto the beach. She edged her way closer to the light.

The men had clattered their way past along the main tunnel and were now in the inner cavern. They were talking quite loudly to each other, laughing from time to time, and there was no indication that they were aware of anyone else nearby. Ian squeezed into the fissure to see what he could see. A powerful lantern lit up the inner cave and he could make out three figures standing in the middle. They appeared to be in no great hurry. One of them swigged from a bottle, passed it to the others, then started to dig. He took a few shovels full, stopped and made a remark, then he dug again and hit rock. The others squatted and scraped some sand aside, then there was heaving and groaning and they finally lifted out a large flat stone. So that's why we didn't find the treasure, thought Ian. It was under a great big stone. He squeezed his way back, "They've got it," he whispered. "We didn't dig deep enough."

"I was right," said Anna. "It must be the stolen jewels.

What can we do? We can't just let them get away with it."

"Phone someone for help," said Tom. Phone Bob, he's the Sark policeman. You've got his number, haven't you?"

"It's no good," said Anna, trying her phone. "No signal."

"They'll be leaving in a minute," said Ian.

"I've just thought of something," said Bart. He whispered his idea excitedly to the others.

"That's brilliant, Bart," said Tom.

"Let's go for it," said Anna.

They scrambled as quickly and quietly as they could to the end of the tunnel and out over the rocks onto the beach. They glanced back to the top of the beach but there was no sign yet of the three men. They dashed down to the rubber dinghy, checked that the oars had been left onboard, then lifted and dragged it down to the water. It was soon afloat. The boys held onto it while the girls clambered in. Then there was shouting from the top of the beach. The boys pushed the dinghy out further then hauled themselves onboard. Bart took the oars and rowed for all he was worth.

The Frenchmen were shouting and running down the beach, one of them waving his spade above his head, the other two clutching metal cases which no doubt contained the stolen jewels. But they were too late, by the time they splashed knee deep into the sea the dinghy was well clear. The man with the spade threw it at the dinghy but it fell short. They shouted and swore at the Islanders and shook their fists but it was all to no avail.

Bart pulled away and the dinghy soon came level with the black boat. They looked her over but there was no sign of anyone onboard. They came alongside and held onto the boarding ladder.

The Islanders were highly elated.

"We've done it! We've done it!" cried Bart.

Anna tried again to phone Bob and managed to get through. "Bob, is that you?" she said. "Quick, we need your help. It's the men from the black boat ..."

The men on the beach were fuming and stamping about, then one of them took off his jumper. There was a splash. "Oh no," said Tom. "One of them's in the water. He's swimming this way."

Anna was still on the phone. "How soon can you get here?" she said. "Right ... Oh, thank goodness ... Yes please, Bob, as fast as you can." She rung off. "They're on the way," she said.

"Come on, everyone," said Bart. "We'd better get onboard."

They climbed up the ladder onto the black boat. Tom was the last to leave the dinghy. He took out his penknife. "Shall I sink it?" he said. Ian and Bart nodded. Tom plunged the knife into the rubber sides of the dinghy and quickly made for the ladder.

The Frenchman in the water was making steady progress towards the black boat. He swam a powerful breast stroke and had a strong and determined look about him. The other men on the shore were watching his progress.

"He'll be here any minute," said Anna. "We'd better pull up the boarding ladder."

Tom helped Anna to pull up the ladder, Ian looked around for something to fight off the Frenchman, and Bart went to check out the wheel house. Seconds later they were startled by the sound of the boat's engine bursting into life. The engine roared and then settled down into a steady rumble. Bart came running from the wheelhouse. "They'd left the keys in," he crowed. "We can drive her away if we have to."

The Frenchman now was approaching the boat. "You mad children!" he shouted at them. "What you think you do? You steal my boat! You in big trouble now."

Ian looked down at him, holding a boathook ready in case the man tried to come onboard.

"It's you who are the thieves," said Anna. "We know what you have in those cases."

"You speak rubbish," said the man. Swimming up to the side of the boat he suddenly lunged himself upwards, grabbed a rope which had been trailing over the side and started to heave himself onboard.

Ian tried to push him back with the boathook but he caught hold of it and pulled it from Ian's grasp. "Right, now I show you," said the man hauling himself up on the rope, "Now I teach you a lesson."

Anna and Shani clung on to each other. "You'd better get inside, girls," said Ian.

Tom looked around for something to throw at the Frenchman. He grabbed a lifebelt from the side of the wheelhouse and threw it with all his might. It hit the man a glancing blow on the head. He dropped back into the water, shouted and swore in French, but recovered and started again to climb up. Then Tom remembered his penknife, he pulled it out and sawed at the rope. In the nick of time it was severed and the man fell back into the sea.

Bart was wrestling with a lever on the anchor windlass. Suddenly he managed to free it and the anchor chain roared down into the water. "Blast!" he said "Wrong way." He pushed the lever back and the windlass started to turn, pulling the chain back in. Bart rushed back to the wheelhouse "It's okay now," he said to Anna and Shani, "We'll soon be out of here." But with all the commotion of the anchor chain, and now the anchor being lifted, the Frenchman in the water could see there was little chance of stopping the children and he started to swim back to shore. Ian and Tom cheered.

To put some distance between them and the Frenchmen, Bart put the engine into gear and steered the black boat out, away from the beach. He looked out ahead and could see boats approaching. Closer in, a blue boat with a white cabin was just rounding the headland and coming straight for them. Bart steered slightly to starboard to avoid a collision. Further out he could see a fast launch approaching across the Great Russel.

On the beach the other two Frenchmen had also seen the boats approaching. They started frantically to search the beach for a way out. They tried in vain to climb the cliff face but soon discovered it was hopeless.

The blue boat, driven by Bob the boatman with the two birdwatchers onboard sped past and headed into the beach. The man in the water gave himself up and the birdwatchers addressed the men on the beach through a loud hailer. "Stop! Stay where you are. Armed police! You are under arrest!"

Epilogue

At first, the Islanders found the reaction to their great adventures was not as favourable as it might have been. The fast launch they had seen approaching from Guernsey had been carrying police reinforcements who had boarded the black boat and been quite surprised to find a crew of children onboard. Bart had been told that his actions more or less amounted to piracy on the high seas, and the rest of them had been advised that they really had no business to get involved in police investigations.

The criminals had been carted off to Guernsey for questioning. The metal cases were found to contain not only the jewellery from the house in Normandy, but also pieces from a string of other burglaries on properties throughout Europe. It was likely that the criminals would be tried in France or Belgium. The Belgian detectives would be taking them back, but first they went back to the hotel with the Islanders. They were surprisingly friendly, now that the thieves had been caught. Inspector Lomers slapped Ian and Tom on the back and said "Hey, junges*, next time we work together!"

Mr and Mrs Riley were mightily relieved to have all of the children back in one piece. "I knew we should have kept a closer eye on them," said Mrs Riley to her husband.

"Anna, why can't you be like other children? Why must you always court danger?"

"It's not my fault, mother," said Anna. "How were we to know they would be coming back for the jewels?"

"I suppose they thought better of it, leaving them there," said Mr Riley. "Or perhaps they thought the coast was clear, and they could take them back to France and have them broken up and sold."

The newspapers, of course, had a field day. "ISLANDERS SMASH INTERNATIONAL CRIME RING," and "POIROT NO MATCH FOR ISLANDERS," were the headlines.

Phil the fisherman had ferried the Islanders back to Guernsey the next day and they told him all about it. "Who would have thought that sort of thing would be going on in Sark?" he said. "You seem to attract these kind of adventures, don't you?"

They said their fond farewells on reaching Guernsey. Anna and Shani had to leave for England on the *Condor*, but Bart stayed with his gran for another week and spent most of his time sailing and fishing with Tom and Ian at Grand Havre.

Glossary

Sark

Sark is one of the smaller Channel Islands, situated in the bay of St Malo, about 8 miles from Guernsey, 15 miles from Jersey and 20 miles from the French coast.

Its land area is approximately 3 miles by 1½ miles (1,274 acres). Population approx 600 in winter, but much busier over the summer season with visitors and day trippers.

There are no cars in Sark, only horse drawn carriages, bicycles and tractors. Even the fire engine and ambulance are pulled by a tractor. The roads are mostly unmetalled and the island is generally unspoilt and peaceful.

Sark is the smallest self governing state in the British Commonwealth. Until recently its government was based on a feudal system that had served the island for well over 400 years.

Victor Hugo

Famous French writer 1802–1885. Author of *Les Miserables* and *Les Travailleurs de la Mer* (*The Toilers of the Sea*). Exiled from France in 1851. Lived in Guernsey, at Hauteville House, from 1855 to 1870.

Victor Hugo was a regular visitor to Sark, staying at the

Dixcart Hotel.
The Toilers of the Sea is of particular interest, being set in Guernsey.

La Seigneurie
Home of the Seigneur (feudal lord) of Sark.

Free holiday
In *Adventures of the Islanders Volume 1*, the Riley family, for their part in catching the villains and for being frequent visitors to the Islands, were rewarded by the Tourist Board with a free holiday.

Islanders
Over the winter, the Islanders decided that Phil should be made an honorary Islander, as they could not have managed, in their crime busting endeavours, without his help.

Russel
The Great Russel is the channel between Herm and Sark. The Little Russel is the channel between Herm and Guernsey.

The song
"Fifteen men on a dead man's chest" from *Treasure Island* by Robert Louis Stevenson (published 1883) is a fictional sea shanty sung by Captain Flint and his fellow pirates. There is only one verse of the original known, although additional verses have been written by others.

Vauban

The Bassin Vauban is named after Sebastien Le Prestre 1633-1707, Seigneur de Vauban, a famous French military engineer renowned for his skill in the design of defensive fortifications.

Duguay-Trouin

The Bassin Duguay-Trouin is named after René Duguay-Trouin 1673 – 1736, a famous French corsair of St Malo. In the early part of his naval career, as a privateer, he captured 16 warships and over 300 merchantmen from the English and Dutch. In the War of the Spanish Succession he captured Rio de Janeiro, previously believed impregnable.

Le Renard

The present day boat is a replica, built in 1991, of the original corsair cutter sailed by Robert Surcouf (1773-1827) a well known privateer sailing out of St Malo.

She has a waterline length of 19 metres, sail area of 450 square metres, and was originally armed with 10 cannon.

Ile de Cezembre

An island of about 44 acres approx 3 miles from St Malo. Fortified by Vauban and by occupying forces during the Second World War. The sandy bay facing St Malo is popular with visiting boats.

Bullet
In their previous adventures, Tom had handed out five spent bullets to the other Islanders as keepsakes.

Dos D'Ane
Pronounced doe dan. The donkey's back.

Shell Beach, Herm
The girls' trip to Shell Beach is covered in *Adventures of the Islanders Volume 1.*

Path to Grande Grève
In the winter of 2009/2010 a substantial land slip covered the path down to the beach. At the time of writing there is no access except by boat.

Flying Christine
The St John's Ambulance launch serving the Bailiwick of Guernsey. Provides first aid and regularly transports emergency cases to the Princess Elizabeth Hospital in Guernsey.

Giant Octopus
There is no record of a giant octopus being found in Channel Island waters although they regularly occur in fishermen's tales. There are many recorded sightings of Octopus Vulgaris which can reach a considerable size (4 to 5ft span) possibly even more.

Junges
Pronounced "yungas." Flemish for: youngsters, lads, kids.